The Early Stuff

Books by Brian Dana Akers

The Hatha Yoga Pradipika

The Early Stuff

The Early Stuff

Brian Dana Akers

YogaVidya.com

YogaVidya.com, PO Box 569, Woodstock NY 12498-0569 USA

"Death Looked Down" first appeared in *New Altars* ©1997
"Djinnetic Code" first appeared in *The Age of Wonders* ©2000
"May/December at the Mall" first appeared in *Chicks 'n Chained Males* ©1999
"Falling Forward" first appeared in *Chronogram* ©2000

YogaVidya.com is a registered trademark of YogaVidya.com LLC.

First edition

Manufactured in the United States of America

∞ The paper used in this book meets the requirements of the American National Standards Institute/National Information Standards Organization Permanence of Paper for Publications and Documents in Libraries and Archives, ANSI/NISO Z39.48-1992.

British Library Cataloguing-in-Publication Data
A catalogue record for this book is available from the British Library.

Publisher's Cataloging-in-Publication Data
Akers, Brian Dana.
   The Early stuff / Brian Dana Akers. — 1st ed.
   Woodstock, NY : YogaVidya.com, 2014.
   viii, [228] p. : 23 cm.
   ISBN 978-0-9899966-5-5 (cloth : alk. paper)
   ISBN 978-0-9899966-6-2 (pbk. : alk. paper)
   ISBN 978-0-9899966-7-9 (ebk.)
   I. Title. II. Akers, Brian Dana, 1958–.

                                        2014946525

Hi Mom!

For Loretta

Contents

Images   1

Island Vacation   13

Arm of Decision   21

The Jewelry Shop   31

Helpful Harry   39

Career Fair   51

Death Looked Down   61

Older Patterns   99

Online   109

Her Big Chance   129

Rollout!   147

Djinnetic Code   155

Job Fair   175

The Ascension of Saint Susan   187

May/December at the Mall   203

Continuing Ed   213

Falling Forward   219

About the Author   227

Images

This is the first story I ever wrote. I started it in Berkeley in the spring of 1991 and finished it in Woodstock in December of 1992. I sent drafts to many friends and relatives for comments and also took it to a workshop conducted by Roger Zelazny. One wag suggested that I merely needed to add either a plot or characterization—preferably both. It went through six complete drafts. I would write a draft, read a "how to write" book, mull it over, then write another draft. I was completely at sea until the third draft.

How does it look over two decades later? Oddly enough, I extrapolated socialist India's bureaucracy just as Finance Minister Manmohan Singh was implementing (for both better and worse) a historic turn to capitalism. But I think I foreshadowed some of Narendra Modi's high-tech campaign of 2014.

"Teach him a lesson! Teach him a lesson!"

The mob surged through the town's bazaar, smashing windows and torching shops. Everyone who could had locked themselves inside and was waiting for the fury to pass. Only one elderly Muslim gentleman, out to buy his day's vegetables, was caught in the open.

"Knock him down!" screamed someone. The front edge of the mob had reached the old man, who was hobbling down a side alley as quickly as he could. A young man snatched his bag of vegetables away, grabbed his shoulders, and spun him into the dirt. The old man landed face down and tried to protect his head with his arms, but the mob was on him. People kicked him and beat him with pipes. When his skull had caved in, they drew back and a policeman came and doused him with kerosene. Someone lit a match. The still-wet blood made a hissing sound in the flames. The smell was awful.

"SitaRam! SitaRam!" the mob cheered. Then it surged back into the bazaar, looking for more shops to burn, others to kill.

Sanjaya was shaking. He had seen the killing from his hotel window above the alley. He had yelled at them to stop, but his voice hadn't been audible above the roar of the mob. Then he had stopped suddenly, lest they think that he, too, was a Muslim.

Sanjaya brushed back his black hair, nowadays ever more tinged with gray. The acrid smoke made him squint, accentuating the slight wrinkles around his eyes. He closed the window and sat in the room's lone armchair.

Until today, these riots were something he had only heard about or seen on a view screen: A Pathan bus driver kills a pedestrian or a cow is slaughtered. A demonstration is held. A bit of violence. Then rumors: the public wells have been poisoned, pregnant women have been raped and disemboweled. Liquor, bribes, and kerosene oil begin to flow. Party activists find out who is who from the locals. Then an orgy of violence. The police are slow to respond at best, joining in the looting and killing at worst. Then the energies are spent. Official inquiries are commenced. Life returns to normal, attackers and attackees living side by side. Until the next wave hits.

What Sanjaya found puzzling was that it should happen here, in this small, remote town that had previously been so peaceful. He wasn't sure what to do. The noise had died down outside, and he wasn't shaking as much now. The old armchair, with its worn fuzzy cloth and busted springs, felt reassuring.

He and his American colleague, Kevin, had been working in the Himalayan foothills for months, racing to complete the final survey of the India Bioregion Map. If they could get it out, it just might make the difference. Kevin had returned to the ashram yesterday, while Sanjaya had broken his journey at this hotel and still had two sets of instruments to collect. If he left now, he could still collect both sets, spend tonight in his tent, then return to the ashram tomorrow morning. He decided to strap on his pack and try for it.

Sanjaya gingerly descended the stairs to the lobby. The desk clerk was gone, so he left the money in an envelope on the front desk. The front door latched on the inside and he let himself out.

The corpse was still smoking slightly, only half burnt. He headed away from the bazaar and uphill. After five minutes, the houses were thinning out. After ten minutes, he was out of town and scrambling up the mountain slope. By late morning, he had made it to his first set of instruments.

One of the goals of the bioregion map project was to account for all bird species. Acoustical prompts made the birds sing; sound activated videocams sent the images to storage. The insect-sized transmitters attached to some birds had all detached themselves on schedule and buzzed back here to their point of origin. The raw data would later be reduced and cross-analyzed with the Thar desert and the Tibet databases for migration information.

Sanjaya was able to locate all the highly miniaturized apparatus and pack them away. He started down the path leading to the second set, taking care where he placed his feet. As always, going down seemed harder on his ankles and knees than climbing up had been.

As he neared the bottom of the mountain, he decided to take a rest. He found a flat boulder near a stream, slid out of his pack, and cracked open his thermos. He poured a cup of cold water, then set it down while he picked up his TouchScreen. Today was the big day in Delhi. The rumblings of war were getting louder. How long can the infobattle be kept at this pitch? If nothing else, he would take in the spectacle.

Kevin, who had that peculiar American mix of sincerity and naivete that Sanjaya found both charming and grating, would sometimes ask him, "The British ruled India with two thousand men. What's going on here?"

That, Sanjaya knew, was the well-established mythology. In truth, the British had always ruled indirectly with the help of many more than their two thousand. By Independence, the number had grown to three million, by 1992 to twenty-four million, and now, today,

August 15, 2011, the one hundred millionth bureaucrat was to be added to the Indian Civil Service.

Sanjaya balanced the TouchScreen on his knees and tuned in Government Channel A. He sipped his cup of water as he watched.

The installation was certainly being conducted with all the pomp that 1.3 billion people could want—Rajput cavalry with lances at the ready, Sikh infantry with blazing red turbans, the stalwart Ravana II fire support system, the gleaming new Pantheon missiles, and of course, elephants. Each elephant wore gold-brocaded head pieces and a red velvet cupola on top for the mahout. Behind the mahout sat a priest, muttering mantras for the benefit of all in the frenzied crowd (some twelve million, according to the announcer). No doubt most were paid ten rupees each and given free transportation, thought Sanjaya. On both flanks of the beasts were hung large video panels displaying 3D martial images from the ancient epics—the Mahabharata, the Ramayana—while the announcer's voice droned on and on about the glories of ancient India, the millennia of history and valor, and how the current regime was the crowning glory of this rich heritage.

The ceremonies had started late because of crowd control problems: twenty-two deaths from sunstroke, thirteen crushed to death, seven dead in police actions. (Touching the MORE button, Sanjaya brought up a clip of the police baton charge. As the wounded crawled away, the officers, proud of their charge, posed smiling for the cameras.) But parts were trimmed so that the main event, the enrollment of the civil servant, would occur at the designated auspicious moment. On schedule, J. T. Pakh, B.A., B.A., B.Sc., M.A., M.A., Ph.D., walked up the wide red carpet, passing between rows of splendidly uniformed soldiers, potentates, and foreign dignitaries, carrying a huge ledger. He ascended the stairs of the reviewing stand and presented his ledger to the president for his signature, thus becoming the Second Assistant to the Associate Vice-Controller for Interagency Coordination, Warangal District.

Sanjaya turned off his TouchScreen and sighed. He stared out in the distance for a moment. The high clouds of the leaden Monsoon sky were dark, yet a clear horizon let in the sun, illuminating the ground. It was almost as if the ground were illuminating the sky. Three white cranes flew overhead. The contrast with the dark sky left him a bit dazzled. He finished his water, repacked, and headed down the trail for the next group of instruments.

By mid afternoon, Sanjaya was hiking through the central section of the survey area, which was one of the few zones where deforestation was not severe. Kevin, his long blond hair hanging out of his sun hat, had transected much of this area to catalog the flora. He had taken both video and physical samples. His data would be compared with satellite data and a twenty-year-old Rapid Assessment Survey.

Sanjaya mused to himself as he walked. It wasn't supposed to be this way, he thought. Gandhi's vision of a self-sufficient rural India had soon given way after Independence to central planning dominated by heavy industry. Some fresh air had begun blowing in the mid 1980s, but by the late 1990s political fragmentation had led to a reliance on central institutions, and the bureaucracy had mushroomed. As the economy spiraled downward, shortsighted politicians played on communal fears to maintain themselves in office. The British hadn't been bad at divide and rule, but the Indians themselves became masters of it. Finally, only the crassest appeals to hate and fear kept the creaking juggernaut in motion.

In the late afternoon Sanjaya passed through a village, now almost deserted due to lack of firewood. It had once been bustling, but as the women had to walk further and further for wood, it became less and less viable. The ashram had once supplied solar cookers to this village as part of its Sustainable Development Programme, but the district collector had, well, collected them. "Wouldn't do to have people too self-reliant, would it? Where would it lead, this self-reliance? Everyone must know their station, this is the essential thing." Only the ashram's position as a Hindu religious institution kept it from being closed down entirely by the bureaucrats. And even then, it couldn't push too hard. Sanjaya pushed on.

By dusk, his feet aching, Sanjaya had come to the last group of instruments and, thankfully, his campsite for the night. He had worked day and—more often—night coordinating dozens of cameras to capture the fauna, producing terabytes of data to reduce. The data would be integrated with other surveys in the watershed. Before it got dark, he quickly checked his instruments. Only the GPS receiver had developed any problems. Everything was ready to be taken back to the ashram. At the ashram, the data would be loaded onto NGO/Net, sent to the supercomputers in Wisconsin for integration into even larger databases, and then, finally, into global simulations.

Sanjaya set up his small cooker and began to prepare his meal. He had developed into quite a fair cook by necessity while doing this fieldwork. Tonight was his final night in the field, so he actually had a small feast of leftovers—nice white rice, chappati, eggplant curry, black gram dahl, mango chutney, and plenty of yogurt for making lassi. Sanjaya checked all his containers.

"Pickle too!" he realized with excitement.

He licked his lips as he stirred his pots. Then he feasted happily.

After eating, Sanjaya retired to his tent and flicked on his Touch-Screen. He found an official spokesman on Government Channel B.

"The Thirteenth Five-Year Plan is nearing completion and will be announced later this month. The main goals will be to eliminate poverty, achieve 100% literacy, and ensure the necessary conditions for a healthy and prosperous life for all citizens. An additional forty-five thousand auditors will be assigned to ensure that all regulations are followed.

"In other news, the Ministry of Steel reports that the joint venture with the Bulgarian Ministry of Steel in Eastern U. P. is behind schedule due to quality control problems. The Ministry is requesting an additional subsidy . . . "

"Enough," thought Sanjaya. He clicked off the TouchScreen and turned off the lantern.

Sanjaya awoke the next morning in a sweat. The riot of the previous morning had troubled his sleep. Not even the lingering aroma of his delicious cooking from last night could get the smell of kerosene and flesh out of his mind. He was anxious to get going. Sanjaya broke camp and headed for the ashram.

It was a long hike, and most of it was uphill. He stopped at lunchtime to catch his breath and to eat a few sweets for energy. He pulled out his TouchScreen to call up Kevin, but could only get static. Strange. He closed it and hurried on.

It was late afternoon as he approached the ashram. He took his final rest and looked across the last small valley whose opposite side led up to the ashram itself. The building lightly capped its ridge, and was a felicitous mix of rooms and hallways, arches and courtyards, gently mixing with the lush gardens tended so lovingly by devotees and guests. It had been built up piece by piece over the decades, as money was sometimes there, and sometimes not. It was beautiful.

After Sanjaya's parents had been killed in a communal riot many years ago, the swami had adopted him and several other orphans and brought them back to the ashram. Sanjaya had many happy memories of growing up there, thriving in an atmosphere of faith and tolerance. The swami had deftly balanced other opposites as well. The ashram had been engaged in environmental activities since the earliest days of the Chipko movement, yet its activism did not disturb its quietism. Its considerable use of information technology somehow did not lead to information overload or anxiety. It let in breezes from many foreign lands, but it was never blown off its foundation. He thought he had bid it good-bye for good when he went to Delhi and then Bangalore for higher education, but this project had brought him back.

After a while, he came out of his reverie and scrambled down the ridge, up the other side, and into the ashram.

He had expected that everyone would be about their serene routines, but instead no one seemed to be around at all. He was wondering what was going on when Kevin suddenly appeared in the hallway leading to the main meditation hall.

"Sanjaya! Heard the news?"

"Not since yesterday. My TouchScreen went inop this morning."

"Not inop. Jammed. Another war panic. Could be for real this time. We've been watching it most of the afternoon."

They headed into the darkened hall together.

People were scattered around the hall in groups of two or three, talking with low and intense voices. People were scared—you could smell their salty sweat. A woman from France was jabbing and cursing her portable phone mercilessly. One man kept bursting into laughter every time someone in his group said something—anything. The largest group was clustered around the large view screen in the front.

Kevin said, "All we can get are the official government news channels. Everything else is jammed, and all coax and fiber links in to and out of the country have been cut."

"He who controls the images . . . " said Sanjaya.

"Controls the receiver of the images," finished Kevin. He paused, then added, "We can't transmit our study."

Sanjaya walked up to the back edge of the crowd and started listening to the news channel. The pompous announcer was vaguely cross-eyed and had one of those silly pencil-thin mustaches.

" . . . These Pakistani aggressions, no doubt aided and abetted by the American CIA, will not go unanswered. The state of emergency will remain in effect indefinitely. All states must submit to direct central rule. The public is reminded that the taking of photographs of airports, bridges, railway stations, military bases, harbors, or other vital locations is strictly prohibited."

The picture shifted back to the parade in Delhi yesterday. But this time it focused even more on the military hardware. The announcer's voice continued.

"India is fully capable of defending itself. Our new Pantheon series cruise missile, using 100% indigenous technology, is fully capable of hitting all targets inside Pakistan."

The missiles looked odd to Sanjaya. He didn't know much about military technology, but the missiles seemed too large, not aerodynamic enough. What was all the apparatus on top? His mind was losing its focus. Another Indo-Pak war. Another distraction to cover policy failures. He needed some air.

"Come, Kevin. Let us go outside," said Sanjaya.

They made their way out of the hall and onto the main deck of the ashram. It looked down the ridge, into the valley and onto the great plains of North India. The daily Monsoon rain had washed the sky and made it clear and still. Two children were at the far end of the deck, playing at being Rama and Sita.

Sanjaya walked out to the railing and rested his elbows on it. Kevin came beside him and did the same.

"I thought we had it in the bag," said Kevin.

Sanjaya ran his soft brown fingers through his hair. He sighed.

"We ran out of time. We were small and nimble, but the sheer weight and scope of the state were too much."

Kevin said, "But we've proved just how imminent collapse of the ecosystem here is! Totally! Conclusively! I honestly thought that if we could get this thing out there, the facade of the regime would finally crack. The people would wake up!"

Sanjaya smiled slightly. Kevin's naivete did not hearten him much now. He was tired. Sanjaya was thinking about the riot, about his parents, about everything. He said nothing.

Kevin continued, "I don't know. Maybe I was hoping for too much. I'm just one scientist." He paused. "I'm going back inside to catch some fresh news. Coming?"

"Go ahead. Later, I will come."

Sanjaya paced a bit. At the far end, the child playing Rama brandished a sword. Sanjaya turned away and walked to the other end of the deck.

Some years ago a well-to-do guest, an astronomy buff, had donated a pair of 20x80 binoculars to the ashram. They were mounted here on a pier, and in the past Sanjaya had often found many hours of pleasure using them. He didn't feel much like using them now, but he also didn't know what else to do.

He started pointing them skyward when a bright blue dot caught his eye. It was close to the horizon, moving east to west. He pointed the binoculars and started focusing in. A man riding an eagle? How could that be? He focused more as he tracked it.

Suddenly, it became chillingly clear. It was the god Vishnu—one hand grasping a club, one hand spinning a discus, one hand holding a conch shell, one hand holding a lotus blossom. The eagle was his mount, Garuda. And both were holographic images projected above a cruise missile headed for Pakistan.

As he followed the blue dot west, he picked up a bright golden dot headed east. He started tracking this one. It was an enormous scimitar, beautiful and deadly, calligraphy etched into its blade and hilt.

By the time he had tracked the scimitar east, the eastern horizon was full of dots—red, green, yellow—many more. He quickly found some of them—Shiva, Kali, Durga. The pantheon. All fearsome images riding cruise missiles. All headed for Pakistan.

The golden scimitar landed with a distant thud.

Island Vacation

This is the second story I wrote, in March of 1993, and it took just two days. I was very relieved to find that—after the protracted labor of my first story— writing could also be quick and effortless. I believe anyone who has ever been on a cruise ship will recognize the setting.

"Cruise ship coming tonight. That's what the Prez says," said Stan.

Matt nudged his sun hat to look up at Stan. Stan had his mirrored shades on, so it was a little hard to tell if he was joking or not. His voice said not. Matt let his hat fall back over his eyes and settled in his canvas deck chair.

"Great. Just what we need. More tourists," Matt replied. "At least they're not coming during the day."

"Yeah. That's always hairy," said Stan.

Stan flip-flopped up the beach toward the resort, beer in hand. He had on one of his all-time loudest shirts. Matt wanted a little more sun before heading in. Even though the weather was perfect almost every day, he still liked to get his morning sun in before he started his afternoon security round. And Stan was great in the morning. Never handed off any big problems to him. Always took care of the morning's problems in the morning. He was like that back in the Air Force, when they were doing the Java Run together. Dependable. When the morning position opened up, Matt talked him into coming out to Gafia.

Now that's a fitting name, Gafia. After Acquisitions had found this little jewel in the Pacific, bought off the natives, and moved them out, Marketing cranked up a helluva campaign stateside. Get Away From It All. Get Away From It All! Get Away From It All!! They poured so much money into the campaign that they decided to rename the island. And it sure is a great vacation spot—warm sun, bright white sand, turquoise sea, the works. A little close to Indonesia and the Philippines, but other corporations beat them to the better locations.

"Time to work, sir!" his beeper said.

Matt got up and headed for the resort. He thought he'd start today's round at the pool.

The pool was trilevel, with waterfalls connecting the pools. Whirlpools were on one side, a live band on the other side, and a bar at the top in the back. Everything seemed fine. He climbed up the marble steps toward the bar. Everything was quiet there, too. He had to smile when he spotted Mrs. Walker.

Mrs. Walker was wearing a string bikini and leaning on the bar. This was her fourth trip to Gafia this year. Her husband is some sort of big-time fixer and arranger. She says we're like family to her and these trips give her life meaning. Her legs were straight and she was bending over at the waist, advertising it. On each cheek of her buttocks was the number 60 in bright red letters. Born in 1960, 60 years old. She was tall, thin, tan, and golden haired. Her second face and body lift had been superb. The only thing a little too perfect about her was her unnaturally straight teeth. They had sort of given him the creeps when he was banging her last night.

He decided to avoid her and started to check out the indoor facilities. He circled round and came through the main lobby. It was a grabber. More waterfalls, trees, birds, animals, and half a dozen party girls in grass skirts. This was their day gig—they did their real work at night. Most had been tourists once themselves. They adjusted.

Matt went through the lobby and into the promenade. The first room on the right was the go-for-it room. In it was just one incredibly fat guy crashed in a beanbag chair, covered with candy wrappers and cookie crumbs. Yep, that's the drill. The room had shag carpeting, beanbag furniture, and four walls covered with cabinets and refrigerators that were always well stocked—but only with junk food. Double-fudge brownies with double-chocolate chunks washed down with a double-cappuccino cola was the latest rage. If you got tired of foraging through the cabinets yourself, a waiter would bring whatever you wanted right to you. If you really had enough, the bathroom had a stomach pump and a vomit pit. It was all guilt free. What are vacations for, anyway?

Matt closed the door and headed down the promenade. Foot traffic was light. Most people spent the afternoons on the beaches or in the water. The next stop was the clinic, or, as he and Stan called it, Hypochondria Central. It was as lavish as the rest of the resort. It had all the diagnostic equipment. Staffed twenty-four hours a day, with the specialists there every afternoon. If they couldn't figure out what was wrong, all the top people stateside were on instant call.

Of course the funny thing was that most of the time nothing was wrong, but that's okay. The staff was always smiling and cheerful and willing to accommodate that request for one final test—just to make sure. Just pop in the credit card and do the test. Hell, the margins were higher here than on the drinks at the bar!

There was just one guy here, too. Seems he was jogging on the beach this morning and his energy level wasn't quite what it usually was near the end of the run. He had checked with his own computer and found 15 possibilities, some of them serious. Better safe than sorry.

Matt continued down the promenade to the theater room. Originally, the room actually had a theater in it. The sound system had been incredible. However, once VR began to take hold, attendance dropped, and the profit-per-square-inch numbers started to look bad. There had been some talk of making it into an orgy room, but right about then everyone started discovering that alcohol and VR don't mix. Guests started actually walking around with their goggles on, bumping into trees, falling down stairs, or walking into the pool when they thought they were flying into the rings of Saturn. He and Stan had to go straight to the Prez on that one. So the theater room became a theater room again, only now every person watched their own separate movie. And the staff was there to make sure no one got hurt. When tourists arrived, the place was jammed.

Matt left the theater room and headed down to the end of the promenade and stepped outside. Gorgeous weather! Someone called his name.

"Matt! Oh, Matt!"

He turned around. Mrs. Walker was seated with a man and a woman near the bar. She was half standing up and waving madly with one arm.

"Matt, come over and meet my good friends," said Mrs. Walker.

He walked over to the table.

"Matt, this is my good friend Jodi. Jodi, Matt is such a sweetie." Mrs. Walker looked at Jodi. Jodi looked at her, then at Matt. They'd been talking. Jodi stood up and pecked him on the cheek. Soft lips. Maybe he'd do her tonight.

"She says you tell just the greatest stories," said Jodi.

"And this is my good friend Harold," said Mrs. Walker.

Harold stood to shake hands. "You got a good thing going here. Great location. Great concept. Great execution. I love it," said Harold.

"Thanks. Anything for you guys," said Matt. He pulled out a chair and joined them.

"See what I mean? So sweet," said Mrs. Walker.

"Mmm," said Jodi, eying him as she sipped her drink. Mrs. Walker was also twinkling her eyes at him. Now he wasn't sure.

"Mrs. Walker here tells us you were in the Air Force, Matt. I was a Navy pilot myself, but I won't hold it against you. Carrier-based ECM. Loved it," said Harold. Now even Harold had a gleam in his eye, but it was more of the old-soldier type.

"You really did the Java Run?" asked Harold.

Matt sat back. He had this story down pat. The guests loved it.

"Yeah. Me and Stan," said Matt.

"Ooh, Stan!" said Jodi. This woman would be defenseless in a poker game.

Matt started his story. "Yeah. You'll recall that at one time the U. S. and Indonesia actually had relations—you could get a visa and travel there, and they could get a visa and travel to the States."

"I remember that. Bali was great," said Mrs. Walker.

"Great," said Harold.

"So we would fly in and land on a strip on Java and…"

"Actually land on Java?!" gasped Jodi.

"Yeah. Actually land and unload. Then it just started to get too hairy. Warlords. Factions. Kidnappers. Disposable people. So we started flying low over the targets and dumping the pallets out the cargo hatch. Then…" Matt paused for effect. He sipped on the Mai Tai the waiter had brought him. Infinite free drinks. This place had the perks.

"Then what?" asked Jodi.

"Then the antiaircraft fire started. The government was completely gone, who got the U. N. seat was in dispute, and antiwesternism set in. Especially anti-Americanism. So we just started flying higher and higher to be safe. The best trick was taking the cargo off the pallets, packaging it in reflective silver, and sending it down loose. It acted as radar chaff that way. That's what I always remember when I think of the Java Run: one million shiny condoms flowing out the rear cargo hatch like powdered snow and floating down into the jungle." Matt touched the Help Me button on his beeper. Now just ten seconds to go.

"Great story," said Harold.

"Oh, so fascinating," said Jodi.

"Duty calls, sir!" his beeper said.

"Oh Matt, must you really go?" asked Mrs. Walker.

"You heard the word. It's been a pleasure chatting with you. I look forward to seeing all of you again. Please enjoy the rest of your stay on Gafia," said Matt.

"I'm sure Jodi and I will see you tonight," purred Mrs. Walker.

Both of them? Matt raised his eyebrows and Jodi giggled. He stood up and excused himself again. Then he continued his rounds.

It was near the end of the dinner show that evening when Stan came up and spoke quietly in his ear, "Now's the time."

Matt got up from his seat in the rear of the room and went with Stan to the Situation Room. It was one of the few places in the resort that was utilitarian. Matt and Stan were the only ones authorized to enter.

"Copter drone up?" asked Matt.

"Up and in position," replied Stan.

"Let's look at it on the monitor," said Matt. He flipped it on and started scanning and focusing. There it was.

"Cruise ship!" said Matt.

"What's the position?" asked Stan.

Matt checked.

"Excellent! The tide should carry the debris away from Gafia. No need to notify the guests or meet the tourists on the beach," said Matt.

"Yep, now's the time," said Stan.

Matt was making his final adjustments. The image was crystal clear. A long, open boat; listing, and taking on water. The passengers were sitting in four rows, two on each side. They were all bent down, furiously praying. One man at the bow was standing, leaning his back on a large cross. His face and both arms were raised to heaven in prayer.

"Filipinos," said Matt.

"The asking-for-compassion routine again," said Stan.

Matt adjusted the cross hairs for the missile on the copter drone.

"Cross on cross," said Matt.

"Cross on cross," said Stan.

"Firing now," said Matt.

One second passed.

"Light show!" exclaimed Stan.

"Light show," agreed Matt.

"Tomorrow on the beach?" asked Stan.

"Tomorrow on the beach," replied Matt.

Arm of Decision

This story grew out of annoyance with the hype that virtual reality was getting in the spring of 1993. It struck me as unlikely that technology and society would evolve along the lines commonly portrayed, and more likely that they would evolve along the lines of ubiquitous computing then being pursued at Xerox PARC.

Defilade in open terrain. Perfect.

Mike had backed his tank over the hill until only his gun and turret would be visible to approaching tanks. Minimum exposure, maximum safety. His laser range finder had surveyed the landscape and entered the values into fire control. If anyone moved up the road, he had them. All his sensors—infrared, acoustic, magnetic, and morphic—had come back on line. His tank's engine was shut down and no longer giving off signatures. The periscope stuck to his pasty white face and sweat trickled down his forehead from his greased, jet-black hair. The vision system took the night away. He was set to deliver more death in the dark. Perfect.

Christ, was he stiff! Most tankers were five foot six or less; Mike was six foot two and maybe even still growing. It was cramped as hell and he had been holding himself in the same position for—hours? days? The chronometer was one system that had not come back up after absorbing the last hit. But he could barely risk blinking, much less take his head away from the periscope.

His forehead was hurting him, but his right hand was really killing him. Driving and firing with the joystick, he had to keep gripping tight. And his left arm! Yesterday, a squash-head shell had hit his tank, flattened and exploded. The shock wave had come through the armor, shaken everything loose inside the tank, and smacked a shell casing into his left forearm. It hurt bad.

Mike kept looking through the periscope at the glowing green landscape. Nothing yet, but they should arrive soon. He checked his heads-up status panel. Mostly good news. The 5E was the ultimate uniperson armored fighting vehicle, the culmination of over a century of tracked fighting-vehicle development. He still had a good selection of anti-armor and antipersonnel shells. The machine guns were working, but the flame thrower was out. He could still generate a smoke screen. Most importantly, the 5 Electronic Measures—Deception, Surveillance, Control, Counter, and Counter Counter—were operating at 75% efficiency or above. His biggest problem was that his AI Assistant, Aye-Aye, wasn't working too well. Or at least wasn't saying anything of much use. And he was stiff.

There! His magnetic sensor showed a large mass of metal slowly coming up the road about 2,000 meters away. The status panel was now awash with color indicators as the target acquisition system locked on.

"Let's see. A shaped-charge shell might prove amusing," said Mike.

"Do it," said Aye-Aye.

He activated the loader and got ready for the recoil.

"Bye-bye!" said Mike.

Mike squeezed the stick's red button. The gun fired. A moment later, 2,000 meters away, the shell hit. A stream of superhot gas penetrated the armor, igniting the fuel, ammunition (and crew) inside.

Alisa sat in meditation, motionless. Her long, thick, blonde hair reached down to the floor, making a lush contrast to her dark blue leotard. Her face, with its creamy complexion and rosy cheeks, was completely relaxed. Her light-blue eyes were closed.

Every Vipassana session progressed for her the same way. First she got comfortable in her sitting position. Then she took some slow, deep breaths to begin quieting down and simply observe things as they are. Then she began to focus on her mind and body processes— not trying to control or reprimand, just slowly letting an awareness evolve. As the feeling began to flow like oil from a lamp, her mind and body lost their estrangement. Then her awareness began to expand beyond her mind/body into her surroundings. She felt a deep delight.

This morning a cool, moist, Pacific-Northwest fog was rolling up the hillside and entering her office. The Japanese screens were open and the fog was wafting in, making her face moist and cool. It felt so good.

Alisa half opened her eyes, closed them, then opened them all the way and drew a deep breath. A smile came to her face. She loved coming out of meditation into her new office. The craftsmanship in the woodwork was really superb. There was a splendid view of the hills, the trees and the lake in the distance. The room could be opened up into a porch or buttoned up against the weather. The fountain outside offered up a soothing water sound. And the information systems were up-to-date, so she could get some serious consulting done when she needed to.

Alisa had gotten the full hierarchy of devices. A large video board hung on the wall for teleconferences. She had told it what she liked and didn't like and now it adjusted its text size, volume and brightness to her preferences whenever it detected a badge she was wearing. Her desk had stacks of video pads on it, each one for a different topic. Alisa had been amazed when she first got them how thin they were making them these days. One night she needed a break and had used them like oversize playing cards and built a big tower. A breeze had blown in and they clattered to the floor while she watched in shock, but they were all undamaged. Scores of little electronic tabs were scattered throughout the room, marking objects and monitoring the environment. She had even broken down under a girlfriend's urging and bought dozens of different badges to go with her different outfits. And all these things talked to each other all the time. They helped make her office a pleasant and easy place to get things done.

She tapped her badge to check for messages. One of the pads changed to bright pink and started humming a lullaby, then, with a lovely lilt, started calling out, "Hello, Alisa . . . Hello, Alisa . . . Hello, Alisa . . . "

Mike jammed it into reverse and throttled it—hard. He had gotten the three tanks, but not before they had gotten his range and called in support. He was waiting for the second platoon to come up the road so he could pick them off when—too late—he heard a fire-and-forget missile screaming at him. It smacked into the left side of his tank and his forearm got banged up again. Thank God for sloped composite armor! Time to scram before another one comes.

The 5E was in open field now, full speed, in reverse. Mike kept the gun pointed toward his old position to cover himself. He could make it to his final fallback position in five minutes. Until then, he was in the open and a big, big target. The status panel showed him down the three antitank shells, and smoke wouldn't do him any good at this speed. All the electronics were hardened, but the 5 Es were still down to about 50% and he was sure he was giving off signatures like crazy now. Three more minutes.

"Oh joy," said Mike.

"Oh boy!" said Aye-Aye.

Three, five . . . six. Six tanks! Target acquisition went crazy trying to pinpoint them. He loaded six shells. The 5E had superior gun stabilization, rate of fire, and platform stability, but this would be his toughest round yet. He squeezed the red button once, twice, a third time. One, two, three of the pursuing tanks gave off satisfying fireballs. Yeah!

Smack! Smack! Smack! Three rounds hit his thick front armor, smashing his head into the periscope each time. Blood started dripping down from his forehead into his eyes and down his cheeks. Target acquisition said it still had them. He squeezed the red button three more times. His right hand felt like a block of ice now. One, two . . . two fireballs.

SMACK! His face was turning to pulp. He stopped the 5E and took dead aim. He squeezed the red button. Fireball.

Mike took a deep breath, cranked his jamming signals to the max, and tried to analyze his situation. The six tanks were history, but he still was in the open and somewhere around here was supposed to be a minefield. Trouble, big trouble, would be showing up soon. Evasive maneuvers? Too time consuming. He decided to head straight for final fallback as fast as he could. He revved the motor and got it to half speed, but no more. The undercarriage had been damaged by that last hit and now he was wobbling back and forth. Maybe four minutes to go at this speed. Mike felt his tank roll over something.

"Pa-tink!"

Oh oh. Transmitter mine.

"You're dead meat now!" said Aye-Aye.

"Are you serious?" asked Alisa.

"Sure, I'm serious. I'll transmit the file. You have authority to proceed immediately. And I mean immediately."

Alisa had picked up the pink pad from her desk, thereby activating it. Dr. Jacobsen had left a message for her. She had called him back to confirm. He confirmed. She set the pad back down and its color returned to neutral.

It's funny how things go. Her psych-history dissertation had been a pretty pro forma affair—enough to make it past the committee, get the degree and enter the job market. But there was a small section on addictions and computers that almost went unnoticed until a journalist's agent had been programmed to comb the nets for that topic. Alisa went on a talk show and gave what she thought was a pretty dispassionate synopsis of her findings. Then some of the few remaining virtual reality hypemeisters did a show touting their position. Shortly, articles, rants, flames, and rambles started appearing on the net. So she weighed in—started appearing on more shows, put some of her more accessible articles online—first with "An Idea of the Future Whose Time Has Passed," then "VR PR," then "Smart Drugs for Stupid People," and finally "Goggles, Gloves and Sheep." These generated enormous reading royalties and led to her being called in as an expert for VR addiction consulting. So she quit the day job, hung up her shingle, and eventually built this house. Hadn't had a VR call in a long time. Hadn't had a fatality in an even longer time.

She picked up another pad and flipped through her VR files to prepare herself. The history of VR was even funnier than how she had gotten into it. For decades it had existed only in science fiction and research labs, then in the late 80's—boom—everyone, *everyone*, was talking about it, even people who couldn't spell microprocessor, much less code for one. It was the combination of the herd mentality and the bandwagon effect that had interested her initially. One of the more ironic things was that VR was always hyped with non-VR technology—computers in the world, not a world inside a computer.

About ten years later, computers became powerful enough to do VR right, and the bubble dissolved pretty quickly. Sure, it's proven useful for going inside cells and exploring distant planets and such, but people preferred enhancing—instead of simulating—the world. It's more human.

Alisa clicked off the pad. The fog was burning off and the sun was coming out. She stood at the window for a moment, feeling its warmth on her face. Delicious. Better get moving. She tied her hair up into a bun and touched her badge.

"Hi car-car. I'm coming."

Mike knew it was coming. He couldn't run. He couldn't hide. He could still fight, but his chances weren't good. The transmitter mine would have called Flying Death—a.k.a. Tank Killer, a.k.a. Helicopter Gun ship 6E—by now. The extra E was for elimination. He waited.

"H-e-l-l-o," said Aye-Aye.

There it was, coming low and slow just over the horizon. Mike cranked up all his jamming to the absolute max. He brought his machine guns to the ready. His main gun would be useless for anti-air. Target acquisition was having fits. The 6E was 100% operational and acquisition couldn't lock on. He switched his machine guns to manual override and pressed his head even deeper into the periscope. The ghostly green tank killer kept floating slowly closer, then stood off just outside of machine gun range. It fired a missile. Then another, then another, then another. They were optically guided, and his jamming wouldn't stop them. Nothing would. This was it. He gripped the joystick. His left arm ached. He braced himself for the impact.

Slam! Slam! Slam! SLAM!

It looked like a fairly ordinary house to Alisa. She quickly double-checked the address Dr. Jacobsen had given her. This was it. She pulled over and parked.

"Bye car-car," she said. The car looked grumpy from having been driven so fast.

Alisa stepped up to the front door and waited one second for it to greet her. Nothing happened. She spotted a little circle on one side of the door and jammed it with her finger. It made a ringing sound, but that's all it did. This was a typical symptom. Alisa tried the handle and it was open. Atypical.

She quickly stepped through the door and looked around. No one. She tapped her badge for info. Nothing. Typical. The house was unintelligent. All of the owner's money was being poured into something else. Normally the badge's operating system would have reconfigured itself to fit the hardware available in its environment and told her what was what.

Alisa strode down the central hall and heard a whirring noise behind one of the doors. She opened it and hurried down the stairs into the dank, dimly lit basement. She turned a corner at the bottom and saw what she expected to see.

The fan noise came from a refrigerator sized cabinet, its fans exhausting bunches of Btus. Must have cost a pretty penny. She bet it could do polygons like crazy. She followed the wires coming out of the back into another room. Alisa saw what she expected to see there, too.

Mike backed his tank over the hill until only the gun and turret were showing. Defilade in open terrain. Perfect. He was stiff and sore as hell, but his systems had come back nicely and he was ready. When the tanks came up the road, he'd blast them.

Alisa walked into the second room and found a tall, lanky young man reclined in an easy chair. She walked up to his side. His right hand was wearing a VR glove and it almost looked arthritic, he was gripping so tight. His left forearm had an IV needle in it, and a huge bottle of IV fluid was slowly dripping away. His goggles were on way too tight and his face was swollen. Sweat covered his forehead. On his shirt was pinned a little hand-lettered sign saying, "Don't unplug me. I'm going for the high score." He smelled pretty rank, but he hadn't injured himself.

This was always the tricky part. One could never really be sure how they would respond and what was the best approach. What little info was in Dr. Jacobsen's file led her to suspect a conversational approach might work.

He peered at the ghostly green terrain through the periscope. The status panel was normal. His forehead was numb with pain. Or had it stopped hurting? Strange, it seemed like the pressure was gone. He blinked.

Alisa loosened the fastener on the goggles and slowly lifted them off his face. The young man blinked several times.

"Did I make it?" croaked Mike.

"Well," said Alisa, giving him her warmest smile, "you virtually made it. Welcome to reality."

The Jewelry Shop

There is a real shop and a real town (and even a real person) behind this story. My wife, Loretta, owned and operated a gift shop when I wrote it in June of 1993. I briefly worked in the advertising milieu in San Francisco and had been playing with ideas for high-tech jewelry for quite some time. The town, the store, the person, the ad business, and the jewelry all came together in this story. If you follow the story closely, you can find the store even today. It's still standing.

The three trainees—two men, one woman—sat on three sides of the table, looking at each other. The fourth chair was still empty, and it was getting late.

They had started out the session with really superb small talk—complimenting each other on their appearance, congratulating each other on surviving the cuts and making it this far, discussing the campaigns they had war gamed. The exchanges were done with all the style and tact they would need to be successful account executives for Henry Steel & Associates, Los Angeles'—hell, the country's! the world's!—number-one ad agency. There were even the obligatory teases and demure denials that one of them would be an associate one day.

It had been very heady, sitting in the penthouse suite, with its 360-degree view of LA, its ultra-lush carpeting, its perfectly lit and displayed sculptures, its immaculate cleanliness and its tropical wood conference table. One chair was empty, waiting to be occupied by Henry Steel himself. None of them had yet met Mr. Steel in person, and they had all been pumped, waiting for him to deliver the final lesson personally. They had done small talk, but now it was late, and they just sat, looking at each other, wondering if they should say or do something.

Just then the door opened and Mr. Steel quickly strode in. "Please stay seated. My lunch appointment was most interesting and unfortunately ran rather long. My apologies."

He sat and pulled his chair up to the table and said with a smile, "I'm quite sure that is the last time I will ever apologize to any of you."

The three of them laughed politely, but also with a trace of nervousness. He was hard to read: middle height, middle weight, outrageously expensive and unbelievably understated clothing; perfect facial, winning smile, gimlet eyes.

"I'm Henry Steel. Like many people out here, that's not the name I was born with; it describes who I am. I'm the number-one ad man on the planet and I want to stay that way. If you further that end, you will be retained and rewarded. If you do not, you will be terminated. If you cross me, the termination will be done with extreme prejudice."

The woman blanched. The man swallowed. The other man stiffened. Henry smiled slightly.

"I would like to repeat in a much blunter form the ten basic principles of my agency's success that you learned in your training. Number One: Clients exist only to be billed. Number Two: Clients are always wrong. Number Three: We don't care if our ads help the client sell or not. Number Four . . . "

Henry Steel couldn't help but recall the lunch he had done today, the tone of the woman's voice in the next booth. He had sat there for a long time after his appointment had paid the tab and left, trying to listen in. It had left him abstracted, but he had done this drill dozens of times before and he knew he could autopilot it. These three looked like fodder, anyway. Where was he?

"Ah, Number Four: Our ads are about us. I like awards," he continued. The woman had risked breaking eye contact with Henry to glance at the man, but she was now focused on Henry again. "Number Five: Needs don't pay, wants do. Number Six: Find a weakness and exploit it. If you can't find one, make one. Number Seven: Target children, the younger the better. Number Eight: Make women unhappy with what they have now—even if it's something you sold them just yesterday. Number Nine: Innovate. And Number Ten: Do the research, then go with your instinct. Any questions?"

The trainees sat there, stunned. This wasn't at all what they had expected. Mr. Steel's public image was so much more . . . gracious.

"Well . . . ?" asked Henry. He was starting to think about his lunch again and wanted to get this over with quickly.

The man cleared his throat and risked a question. "Would you give us an example of innovation?"

"Gladly," said Henry. "As you know, we must constantly look for new transmission channels for our ads. Our office in Omaha has been working with an agribusiness client to complete the ad/food cycle. They've just completed a new hotdog package and logo. The consumers open the package and find the company logo on every hot dog. They eat the hot dog. The chemicals in the logo create a strong aftertaste with every burp that makes them want to eat more—the advertising continues. Finally, when they defecate into a standard chem toilet, a microprocessor embedded in the logo is triggered by the chemicals and plays the company jingle. Kids love it. Thus, we have them eating, tasting, and shitting our ads. That pretty well sums up our business, wouldn't you say? Dismissed."

The three thanked him for his wisdom and promptly got up and left the room. Henry stood up and walked to the windows. Another crystal clear day. He sighed. Unfortunately, that pretty much did sum up his business. He was bored and needed some innovation himself.

He couldn't get over the conversation he had overheard at lunch. The tone of the woman's voice had just sent chills through him. She had kept telling her companion that this was it, really it, the real thing. It was what everyone was really looking for, what everyone really wanted. It was it. And she wasn't faking it—Henry was sure about that.

Henry thought about it. He couldn't do the research. If anybody found out he was serious about something like this, he was finished—no one would fear him, his empire would start to crumble. And just in case this wasn't really it, he still wanted his empire. What to do? What else? He decided to go with his instinct. He tapped his wrist strap.

"Have my plane ready and scheduled for a flight tomorrow from LAX to La Guardia with a ground car programmed for upstate."

It was overcast Tuesday, with rain threatening, as his car crested Mill Hill Road and turned right and parked in the municipal parking lot. Henry had changed from his business suit to what he hoped was typical tourist attire on the way from the airport. He didn't want anyone to recognize him.

Henry got out and took his bearings. Once he was headed upstate, he had called up a map of town—it was something any tourist would do. He walked past the newly installed public toilets, then turned left on Rock City Road and walked to the intersection. The village green was across the street to his right. A group of teenagers and a few street people were hanging out on the green. They were dressed very archaically—wild patterns of bright colors, wide bottom pants, lots of beads. Henry wondered if it was by choice or by law to preserve the flavor of the town. And it certainly did have flavor. More than flavor—mystique. Maybe this still was the source, the very epicenter of what he was looking for. He almost felt as if the festival was still going on.

Henry crossed the intersection and walked down Tinker Street, keeping the weirdness of the village green across the street. He paused briefly at every shop as he passed. The woman at the restaurant had said it was just past the green, in the heart of town. He crossed a driveway and abruptly stopped. This had to be it.

The shop was set back from the street, with a catching window display and a charming garden. The sign on top said Talismania, the name spelled out over and over again with a rainbow sparkler. Large rain drops started to fall. Henry took a deep breath and stepped inside.

The store felt old, like a pioneer house endlessly renovated. The wood floors were freshly oiled but still worn looking. Cases of jewelry lined the walls. There seemed to be only one other customer. Good. He started to look at the different pieces. They were very active, very complicated pieces and difficult to really get a handle on.

"I'll be with you in a second, hon," called out the saleswoman, a tall redhead.

"I'm fine," said Henry.

"You don't look fine to me," yelled the saleswoman.

Henry was taken aback. Wasn't this woman ever trained? No one ever talked to him like that. Did she know who he was? No, and she couldn't. He would have to take it.

The saleswoman rung up the other customer, then came over. "You need a more flavorful life, that's what you need," she said.

"How do you like this piece?" She held up a gold bangle bracelet that gradually shaded from yellow to white.

"You like Chinese food? This right here is a sweet and sour bracelet. Yellow is the sweetest and white is the sourest, with all the shades in between. You feel like a snack, it's right on your arm!" She was standing a little too close, waiting for him to say something. She was also having a little trouble breathing—probably asthma.

"Ah, no, I don't think so," said Henry.

"Let's see. We got lots of unisex necklaces right now, with all the latest tech, too. Here's a fine piece. Look at this one, hon." She was driving him crazy with this hon stuff.

She pulled out a gold chain necklace. Every other link had a pink tourmaline set in granulated gold.

"This one has an Etruscan inspiration. Each stone gives a different fragrance. You can use it for perfume or medicinally for aroma therapy." She leaned down and whispered in his ear, "This stone is musk. The women will swarm you," and elbowed him in the ribs.

Henry took half a step back and rubbed his rib cage. "No, no that's not quite it."

"Here we go, shy guy." She lifted out a twisted choker with matching earrings. Multiple strands of pink baroque pearls were accented by gold funnels with black enamel detailing.

"Isn't this a nice torsade? A woman would love to receive this. The earrings deliver perfect stereo sound, either audible or subliminal. Get your Ph.D. without even knowing it! Snap them one way, and the wearer hears it; snap them the other way, and other people hear the sound. The necklace holds about 200 gigabytes of audio and a pretty powerful little amplifier."

Henry didn't say anything. She paused and touched his forearm.

"Ok, hon, tell me—is this for you or someone else?"

"It's for me," said Henry.

She glanced at him sideways and stepped over to another case. Henry looked out the window. It was raining harder now, but another customer could still walk in at any moment. He would have to make his move pretty soon.

"You read history? Ever hear of mood rings?" She plumped a large heavy gold ring with angled rows of channel-set baguette diamonds into his palm.

"This doesn't reflect your mood, it creates it. Can fix up a bad day real quick. Don't like somebody? Change the setting and shake hands with him—that'll do it!" she cackled. "You can also monitor your body functions, administer transdermal drugs, the standard stuff."

Henry looked at it.

"Well, I got just one more idea and that's this," she said, holding a necklace up to her chest. A small round video screen was bezel set in gold and accented with pavé-set diamonds and cabochon sapphires.

"In the old days, this center piece would be a coin or a cameo. With the video screen, you can put a whole photo album inside." She squeezed the side a few times. "See this girl with her leg in a cast? That's my wounded inner child!" She cackled twice as hard as the last time.

Henry cleared his throat. "These are all very beautiful, very state of the art. Actually, I'm not looking for anything quite so glamorous. I was wondering if you might have something a little more, um, unique to this area, more of a local . . . "

"Well, why didn't you say so, hon?" She went to the front counter and pulled out a small, plain-looking ring.

"LP&H—our store special. We've upgraded the software many times, but the price hasn't changed in three-quarters of a century."

"How much is it?" asked Henry.

"Hon, in Woodstock, Love, Peace and Happiness is still $19.69."

Henry paid her, tucked the package under his arm, and stepped out into the rain.

Helpful Harry

This story came to me in August of 1993 as I was turning off my reading lamp. I lay there in the dark for a couple of minutes, then turned the light back on and made a page of notes. A few days later I sat down and wrote the entire story in one sitting. I hope you find it amusing.

After collecting a few rejection slips, I submitted this and the following story to the writers workshop expertly run by Adrienne Foster at ConAdian, the 52nd World Science Fiction Convention. I collated the suggestions offered and created "Djinnetic Code," which appears later in this collection. Compare the two stories to see how educational a workshop can be.

Crack! The auctioneer's gavel came down hard, closing the sale.

The grinning buyer took his card up to the table to complete the paperwork. The banker's representative was only too happy to help, having said several times that morning that selling the house would only just begin to make the bank whole. The two dozen or so others in the small crowd began to disperse. George was sitting under the big maple tree on his front lawn, watching it all.

Things sure happen fast these days, George reflected. His wife couldn't bear to watch. She had taken their two daughters to her mother's house. He wasn't sure if he would see them again soon and he really couldn't blame her.

It was a beautiful last day of June—deep blue skies, cotton puff clouds, vibrant green trees. The house they had just lost was a cute white split level. His office was at one end, his wife's was at the other, and there was plenty of space in the backyard for the kids. Just one month ago today everything was great. George pulled another tender shoot of grass to nibble on. Things certainly do move fast these days.

The banker's rep and the buyer finished up their work. The buyer was ignoring him, but the rep was looking him over, probably wondering if George was going to cause trouble. George managed a friendly wave and half a smile. The rep shrugged and decided to leave him alone. They both drove off. George didn't really blame them, either. They were just doing their jobs. It all started one month ago at the mall.

Memorial Day was unusually hot and humid, so the family had voted to head for the air conditioning and spend the day shopping. Unfortunately, it seemed just about everybody else had the same idea—the mall was packed. Their daughters started squabbling after about three stores, so George had taken the six-year-old and his wife the older one. Everyone would rendezvous later at the car.

The two of them strolled through Food Alley. George bought an ice cream cone for her and a pretzel shrimp cup for himself. He was always amazed that they could still come up with new ways to prepare pretzels after all these years. They kept walking until they came to a software store.

"Honey, Daddy wants to go in here for a minute," said George. His daughter sized up the situation immediately.

"Buy me a game?"

"Sure. And be careful with the ice cream."

She streaked back to the game display. George started out with the magazines. "The 986's Are Here!" screamed one headline. George turned down the volume and moved on to the book section. ATM to the desktop seemed a hot topic. After a bit he went to look at the software at the front counter. He didn't see anything there until one package caught his eye—Auto Agent, by some company he hadn't heard of before. He picked it up.

"Great program! A lot of our customers have been very happy with it," said the clerk behind the counter.

"Uh-huh," said George. He learned long ago not to trust software salespeople—especially eighteen-year-olds in bright red vests.

"No, seriously," said the clerk. "We have a Memorial Day promotion on it. Twenty percent off and a money back guarantee right from us." He rang the register and gave the cash drawer a few reassuring pats.

George looked at the box. "A personal assistant inside your computer . . . virtually autonomous program that does what you tell it to . . . runs in the background." George looked back up. The clerk was beating the counter like a drum kit. Someone coughed behind him. His daughter pulled on his pants leg and gave him her selection.

"OK, I'll take these two," said George.

"Good choices, sir. I play that game all the time on weekdays," said the clerk.

The clerk rang up the sale and gave George the bag. They headed back up Food Alley and then to more stores to kill some time. As they left the software store, George heard a voice trailing off, "Great program! A lot of our customers have been very happy with it . . ."

It wasn't until later that week that George sat down at his computer and cracked open the shrink wrap on Auto Agent. He deactivated his virus protection, then popped in the shiny disk and started through the installation procedure.

A picture box opened on the left of the screen; a scroll bar on the right. A line of text said, "Choose how you want your agent to look."

George started clicking on the scroll bar. Different faces started appearing in the picture box: male, female, androgynous, dark, light, formal, casual, on and on. A very cute Asian woman appeared.

"Hmm," thought George, "No, better not. Too distracting."

He kept clicking until he came to a fairly young, nondescript white male with a helpful look on his face. George decided to go with this guy for now. He clicked the OK button.

"Choose a name for your agent," said the installation program.

"He looks like a Harry to me—Helpful Harry," thought George. He typed in just "Harry." The man in the picture straightened his shoulders and looked more attentive.

"What is your occupation? (Supply details)," asked the installer.

George typed in "viral engineer" and tried to remember what folder his résumé was in. He finally located it and appended it to his job title. Harry furrowed his brows and looked intrigued.

"Do you want your agent to be always on?"

"Hell, yes!" said George aloud, "I've worked hard for my software. It's time for my software to start working hard for me." George clicked OK. Harry looked happier.

"One of your agent's talents is combing online databases to prepare informative reports customized just for you. If you would like this service, please enter your access codes now."

This was sounding better and better. George had long ago given up on trying to keep up with everything in his field. On those days he went into the lab, one of the other researchers frequently brought up some new development he hadn't heard of. Maybe Harry could help him turn the tables. He located his access codes, credit information, and bank accounts. He typed it all in. Harry was positively smiling now.

"Do you want your agent to do his very best and bother you as little as possible?"

This struck George as a no-brainer. Of course he did. Who would want less than the best of someone's efforts? And the whole point of an agent was to take as much of the load off one as possible. George clicked OK. Harry beamed.

There followed a few more questions—what timbre of voice was desired, what type of attire, and so on—and then George clicked OK for the last time. The disk drives whirred for a while as the installation was completed. George popped the disk out.

Harry appeared in the upper left corner of his screen and said, "I'm just so happy to be working for you, George. Anything at all, just ask. You know, I've already noticed that the organization of your hard disk is suboptimal. Want me to clean it up a bit?"

"Sure," said George. He was old enough to still be a little surprised when a program talked to him, but young enough not to be too surprised. "I'll check back with you after dinner to see if you have any questions."

George got up and headed for the kitchen. He swore he could almost hear Harry whistling while he worked. "Better him than me," thought George.

That evening, George sat back down at his computer to look at what Harry had done. He was very impressed. This way of arranging things just made so much sense. Why hadn't he thought of it earlier? There were even a couple files flagged for his attention that he had lost track of months ago.

"Harry, are you there?" asked George.

"Yes," replied Harry. His picture instantly appeared in the corner of the screen.

"Great work," said George.

"Oh, I'm so glad you like it!" gushed Harry. "I also prepared six alternates, just in case you didn't like this one."

"No, this is fine. I'm going to bed in a while. Do you think you could scan through the net and put together something for me to read over breakfast—a little news, some sports, latest developments in my field, and so on?"

"Absolutely!" said Harry. "That's one of my specialties. Behind every great scientist is an agent. I'm sure your colleagues will find you more and more impressive as I learn about your field."

George said good night and headed for bed. This time, Harry definitely was whistling.

***

June became the happiest and most exciting of months for George. The morning after installing Harry, he went into his office and found a dozen pages in the printer's output tray. He thanked Harry and headed for the kitchen. His wife had already gotten the kids off to school and was skimming through a magazine while she drank her juice. George poured himself a bowl of cereal, sat down, and started going though Harry's newspaper.

"Game Six tonight," said George.

His wife rolled her eyes, but said nothing. George kept eating his cereal.

"Another coup in Africa. The president went to the meeting of the Organization of African Unity to give a speech and back home the air force strafed the presidential palace and tanks surrounded the TV station. When the cat's away . . . " said George.

"That's nice dear."

George kept reading. A researcher in Australia had just announced the results of his latest experiments on guanine bases. Harry had made a note that the guy didn't seem to be tipping his full hand. Furthermore, Harry had done a little checking and it seemed to him like there were interesting possibilities for new work on sequence spaces. George mulled it over.

"I'm going into the lab today," he declared. His wife looked up at him and blinked.

"That's nice dear. Don't bring any viruses home with you. And don't forget to change out of your pajamas!"

George wound his way through the corporate campus and checked into his building. The lab manager was standing in the lobby with his damn clipboard chatting up the receptionist. He did a double take when George came through the door.

"George! So happy to see you in the AM! Taking a break from the wife and kids to put in a little work time?"

George mumbled something about always doing his best as he strode past. The jerk had given him a lousy 3% on his last review. He was single and wanted to be Vice President of R & D some day, so he was always pushing people to produce and screw the family life. George's old manager before the last reorg was much better. If there's anything to this sequence spacing idea, el jerko sure as hell wasn't going to get the glory.

George turned the corner and walked into his lab. Two of his colleagues were there and they did double takes too when he walked in. "OK! So I like to work at home in my pajamas! Give me a break!" thought George. He tried to act nonchalant. He took out an edited summary of the Australian research.

"Have either of you heard anything about this?" he asked. They both looked at it.

"Nope. Not me."

"Me either. Doesn't look too promising."

"Yeah, I don't think so either. Just thought I'd check. Always like to keep up with the latest developments, you know," said George. The two looked at each other, then looked at him.

"Sure you do, George," said one.

George put in some more face time to allay suspicions—going through notes on his desk, tinkering with some apparatus—then went back home. He had work to do.

Some days later he was sitting at his computer when Harry appeared on the screen.

"Hello, George. I have something for you! I've noticed that your BioCad program is not really up to snuff on Double-strand RNA viruses. I found a shareware module on a bulletin board in the Netherlands that should do the trick. Want me to load a demo for you?"

"Sure!" said George. This was great. With every passing day, Harry was able to figure out his needs better and better. George also thought he was definitely onto a discovery—possibly a rather significant one. It was all due to Harry. Every time George asked him to do something, he gave it his best shot. The best part was, Harry was doing things that George didn't even think to ask.

A full color animation of a reovirus came on the screen. George watched it go through its life cycle. Very spiffy. This could cut hours off his simulations.

"Load it up!" George told Harry.

"Yes sir!"

"Say, I have something I'm wondering if you can help me with," said George.

"Anything I can possibly do, I will," said Harry.

"As you know, I've been following up on your leads about sequence spacing. I'm getting close to building my first simulation. I'm very excited. I was wondering if you could do a little preliminary work—sequence the genome, develop some preliminary possibilities and so on. Take your time. The family and I are going away for the weekend. You don't have to print it out till Monday morning."

"Sure thing, George!" said Harry.

George puttered away for a while longer; sending some email, making a few notes to himself. Right before he got up to load the car, Harry came back on the screen. He seemed a little nervous. In fact, he even seemed to be sweating a little.

"George? I don't think this is going to fit on your hard disk. Can I use the computer at the lab; maybe some net resources?"

"Sure," said George. "Don't worry about it. I'm sure you'll do your best."

Harry looked a little calmer and disappeared. George and his family left for the cabin on the lake. Not many people liked to rough it these days, but George still did. No phones, no TVs, just the lake and the wind. Gave him time to think things through. What exactly does one wear to accept a Nobel Prize, anyway?

***

They came back Sunday evening to the hell that was to be their life for the rest of June. A squad car was in the driveway and yellow police tape was wrapped around the house. An officer was sitting on the front steps, reading and waiting. They pulled in the driveway.

"What the hell is going on here?" screamed his wife.

The officer closed his book and stood up. "It seems you are in a bit of financial difficulty. Perhaps Harry is the best one to explain it to you."

"Harry?!" said George.

They all rushed in to George's office. George sat down at his computer. He said very firmly, "Harry, what is going on here?"

After a delay, Harry appeared in his window in the corner of the screen. He looked awful. He hadn't shaved in three days. Probably hadn't bathed or slept either. His forehead was covered with bruises. Somebody had beat him up pretty bad. He licked his lips and started to speak.

"Tried the best I could, George . . . too many possibilities. 410,000 possible sequences . . . needed more computing power. Lab computer also too small . . . needed full network resources . . . gave your bank info . . . started tying up hundreds, thousands, millions of processors. Tried to hide who I was . . . who you were . . . ran up a huge bill . . . tried my best." Harry's voice trailed off.

"It was quite something," said the officer. "Computers all over the world started getting sluggish. Nobody could trace it. Needed to unleash some special agents of our own, if you catch my drift. When they finally found him, they had to be a little rough, I'm afraid. He must have really liked you. He was determined to do the best he could."

The officer lowered his voice. "I suggest you deinstall him. He could traumatize your whole system."

The rest happened very swiftly and inexorably. They were impossibly deep in debt. Yes, they were responsible for it. Yes, the creditors wanted whatever they could get their hands on. No, the software company that published Auto Agent was no longer in business. Yes, the software store in the mall would refund the purchase price, but wasn't liable for anything else. The clerk said the program worked as described when installed properly.

George sat under the big maple tree on the front lawn, wondering. A month ago, everything. Today, nothing. House, family, gone. He even missed Harry a little bit. The guy was just doing his job, really. George had groveled before the lab manager to keep his position, but his wages would be garnished from here to eternity.

He just wondered if there wasn't some way to retrieve the situation. Perhaps he could go on a talk show and create a wave of sympathy and donations. Nah! Those shows featured freaks, and he was a viral engineer.

Maybe he could write a book about it—spice it up, make it a thriller. But he didn't know much about writing, and he certainly didn't know much about publishing. And who was left to help him?

It was just about then that the idea that was to make him wealthy and world famous crept into his skull. Who knew best how it all happened? Who looked so dejected when he was deinstalled?

Who, in point of fact, was already an agent?

Career Fair

I wrote this story in October of 1993 as IBM was undergoing massive lay-offs worldwide and particularly in their operations here in the Hudson Valley. Moreover, there was a global recession and the Superconducting Super Collider had just been canceled. And, yeah, I used to be a typesetter.

Hang on! It's only going to get worse. (Or is that better? No, I think worse. No, why not waaay better? No, . . .)

"We're going to the fair! Daddy says we're going to the fair!"

"Be gone, short stuff," said Brent, flicking a spitball at his little sister. "Never enter my abode without my express permission."

"Can I come in?" asked Audey.

Brent let her writhe a moment, trying to hold her excitement in. "OK, but you must assume the proper pose of obeisance to your elders," said Brent.

"Forget you! Daddy just called. We're all going to the county fair this afternoon. He's coming home from work early. He said it's our last outing together before you go off to college. We get to eat there, too. I'm having cotton candy for dessert!" said Audey.

"Smart nutritional selection, my diminutive sibling. You may depart. Please bow and scrape appropriately as you leave."

Audey stuck out her tongue and knocked over one of Brent's models as she tore out of the room.

Ahh, college cannot come too soon, thought Brent. When one scores double 750s on the SAT, every contact with mere mortals becomes painful. It was just a question of weeks before he assumed his rightful place among the . . . the . . . Brent grabbed his well-thumbed dictionary. The cognoscenti. Lucky that one wasn't on the test! And the fair would be cool to go to one last time: ride the rides, laugh at the freaks, scarf the corn dogs. Brent looked at his Space Shuttle desk clock. Better start getting ready to go.

Dad swooped into the driveway and bounded up the front steps. "Ok guys, I'm home! I'm going to shower and quick change and then we're off," he said, disappearing into the bathroom.

Audey was running around squealing and looking for her shoes. Brent was sitting on the couch, coolly flipping through his astronomy magazine. He had his T-shirt tucked in and the safety strap on his glasses adjusted. He was set.

It wasn't easy being a single father, but Dad did his best. He had dropped out of his engineering program to put Mom through graduate school. When Mom split to find herself in California, Dad got custody. He went to his purchasing manager job every day, then came home every night and cooked and cleaned and collapsed. Brent had some appreciation for what Dad was going through. He just wished Dad would quit saying, "One down, one to go" every time someone asked about Brent's college admission.

Dad came out wearing sandals, Bermuda shorts and a polo shirt. Audey found her shoes. Brent stood up and brought his magazine to read on the way. The three of them jumped in the car and headed for the fair grounds.

"What shall we do first? Eat?" asked Dad.

"Rides!" said Brent.

"Prizes!" said Audey.

"Ok, we'll eat first, then do rides and prizes. Stay close to me Audey, I don't want you getting lost."

Dad had reason to worry—the place was thronged. They zig-zagged their way through the cars in the hayfield that was serving as a parking lot. It was a crush at the gate. Dad paid and got a program. He looked it over.

"There's a pretty good country singer at the bandstand tonight. Want to go?" asked Dad.

Brent started making gagging and vomiting sounds.

"Okay, forget it," said Dad.

It was a great lazy, hazy, happy summer afternoon at the fair. They tried to do it all—and more or less succeeded. They sat in a big tent and ate foot-long hotdogs smothered in ketchup, mustard, relish, onions and sauerkraut. Brent had a corn dog for dessert. He started to burp after every bite to demonstrate his total appreciation for the fine art of corndog making, but the mother of the family on the other side of the table started glaring at them and Dad told Brent to stop it. Brent then started farting after every bite, but it was too loud in the tent for anyone (except maybe Audey) to hear it, so he stopped. Audey got her cotton candy for dessert. Just like every year, Dad told her to be careful with it, and, just like every year, she ended up totally sticky. The three of them went on the Ferris wheel together (boring, but nostalgic, thought Brent), and also the Cups. Dad and Audey watched as Brent rode the Zipper—twice. Brent was a little woozy coming off, but he gave the thumbs up and they proceeded to the bumper cars. Brent got in one car and Dad took Audey in another. Brent was merciless and fairly certain he caused three cases of whiplash. Later, Dad even shot a few hoops and won a small troll for Audey, which sent her delight indicator into the red zone.

As evening came, they were walking through the 4-H tents, admiring the prize-winning produce and livestock. Audey was having fun wrinkling and holding her nose at the smells. There wasn't a huge amount more to see. Dad liked to avoid the sleazy part of the fair when he was with the kids, (although he claimed to have stories he would tell Brent someday). They decided to head down one of the arcade aisles to get back to the car. They were stepping over cables and dodging the crowd when they heard a shill shouting out.

"Yo free-lan-cers! Yo free-lan-cers!"

Brent and Dad stopped and looked at each other. What was this guy talking about? They got a little closer.

"Yo free-lan-cers! Yo free-lan-cers! You have your shit together?"

The shill was a black teenager in torn jeans and a T-shirt. Brent thought at first that he was a fool for Christ, but the rap wasn't right. Freelancing? Brent noticed the shill was holding a stack of flyers in his hand. Brent darted up and asked for one.

"Here you go, my man. Three booths down on the left. And take your old man," said the shill. Then he started his rap again.

"Yo free-lan-cers! Yo free-lan-cers! Was your company loyal to you?"

Brent scurried back with the flyer and showed it to Dad. It read, "Dr. Darwin's Career Estimation Service. I guess your career or you win a prize." In smaller type below, it continued, "Will predict the future of your career for a small additional fee."

"Let's do it," said Brent. "Two years ago a guy tried to guess my weight and blew it. That's how I got my desk clock."

Dad looked a little worried. He didn't love his job, but he loved the paycheck. And he sure as hell needed it, too. He wasn't sure he wanted to know the future of his career.

"Well, maybe if Audey wasn't with us . . ." said Dad.

"I'm not tired!" chirped Audey.

"C'mon Dad. I'm sure this guy's no good," pleaded Brent.

Dad gave in and they walked down three booths and crossed over to the left side. A man dressed in a nineteenth-century suit, complete with stiff collar, top hat and walking stick was holding forth on a small platform. Behind him was a door with a dinosaur on each side forming an arch.

" . . . yes it is, it is, yes, it is indeed survival of the fittest, that's what I'm saying. It is a jungle out there, my friends, and it's getting worse all the time! Restructuring. Automation. Globalization. ANY ONE of these could send you on a very long and unpleasant ride on the Down Escalator of our society."

The barker gave the crowd a terrifying look. "You don't know what's coming at you next, or from which direction. Everything is just OUT OF YOUR CONTROL. You have to be prepared, or you'll end up like one of these!" he said, and smacked one of the dinosaurs with his walking stick.

Just then, two men bearing a stretcher came out of the door and down into the crowd. They were carrying a man dressed in a blue suit, white shirt, red tie and black shoes. He must have fainted inside. "IBMer" Brent heard someone say. "The bigger they are, the harder they fall," said another.

"Now what is the best way to avoid that sad gentleman's fate?" the barker continued, gesturing to the departing stretcher. "INFOR-MATION! Yes! Information. Not brawn; brains. Knowing what's what. Having a goddamned clue, ladies and gentlemen. And the best way to do that?" He paused.

"Dr. Darwin's Career Estimation Service! Now, I am not Dr. Darwin, no siree. That very wise and compassionate gentleman is behind that door waiting to help you. I am merely trying to give you the vision and courage to help you help yourself by stepping through that door. You won't regret it, no siree, no."

Brent looked up at Dad. He was sweating. Brent had never seen such a panicked look on his face. Dad really didn't want to know, but he knew he would be better off if he did.

"This place is creepy," said Audey.

"This might be worthwhile," said Dad. "Let's give it a shot, then go straight home." They walked up the steps and through the door.

"Now there's a man not afraid to embrace the future! Even taking his two kids. Do I have any other courageous, productive citizens?" asked the barker.

It was dim inside, kind of like the spook house where the carnies had reached out and touched them that afternoon. They climbed up three steps, turned left, and walked down a short hallway. A middle-aged guy was standing behind a rope, waiting his turn. A woman was sitting in the center of the room, with spotlights shining on her. In front of her was a very small midget, sitting in a chair placed on a table. His head was much too large for his body. A gigantic-seeming can of soda was next to his chair, with a long straw sticking out of it. He could sip on the straw without picking up the can.

In the shadows to the left and behind the midget was a contortionist. He would change positions suddenly and without warning; wrapping his legs behind his head, bringing his feet beneath his chin. His eyes were rapacious. To the right and behind the midget was a fat lady—very fat. Brent figured six hundred pounds, at least. She had a huge wart on one of her necks. Totally gross. Next to her was a thin man—very thin. Probably around seventy pounds. He looked like you could break his arms and his legs with your bare hands. I wonder if they're married, thought Brent. The midget was talking.

"Well, stand up madam, let's have a look at you."

The woman was tall, platinum haired, and wearing a trench coat. She opened up the coat and spun around on her high heels, revealing that she was wearing only a red and white polka dot bikini underneath. The red in the dots matched the red in her earrings, and in the lipstick on her full, perpetually pouting lips. Her muscles were finely sculptured. Her skin, flawless.

"Oldest profession," said the contortionist, leering.

"No doubt about it," said the fat lady.

"None at all," said the thin man.

"I must agree," said the midget. "Madam, you are a prostitute. And a very successful one, I suspect. If I am correct, please leave ten dollars with the thin man as you leave. As to the future of your profession, I can assure you it is secure—no need for a second fee."

The woman stripped a ten off a large wad of bills and winked at the thin man when she handed it to him. The fat lady jabbed him in the ribs with her elbow and snatched away the ten dollars.

"Next, please," said the midget.

The middle-aged man ahead of them unhooked the rope and sat down in the chair.

"Doesn't look happy," snarled the contortionist.

"Thinks he's underpaid," growled the fat lady.

"Accustomed to being fat, happy and stupid," spat the thin man.

"Sir, I understand the job market today is very treacherous," said the midget. "But an unhappy demeanor will only make matters worse."

The man replied, "My wife said I should come here. I told her not to worry, there will always be a demand for quality. My shop just isn't keeping up to date. What can I do?"

"Pick up the clue phone."

"We are all freelancers. Some of us just don't know it yet."

"You and the shop are not the same. Don't confuse them."

"Quality, sir," said the midget, "is recognizable only to a few— and fewer still are willing to pay for it. I can only conclude that you are a typesetter."

The man looked stunned.

"Welcome to Earth."

"Lunch meat."

"'Fix me, I'm broke.'"

The midget continued, "For an additional ten dollars, I will tell you the future of your profession. I suggest you wake up and smell the coffee today, so that you will have food for breakfast tomorrow."

"Go ahead," said the man.

"As a distinct profession, your livelihood is about to become extinct. Gone. It will merge into the larger information industry. True professionals don't wait for a pink slip. You must adapt or you will be unemployed. Please leave twenty dollars with the thin man."

The man grumbled, left the money, and walked off. The fat lady snatched the money again.

It was Dad's turn. This was too weird. Brent wasn't sure what Dad was going to do. Audey clung to Brent. Dad sat in the chair.

"Middle management."

"Getting it from above and below."

"Like swimming in a pailful of spit."

"Actually, I would like to ask you a question," said Dad. "Weren't some of you in the freak tent years ago?"

"Yeah," said the midget. "That was easy work. Just sat there and answered a few dopey questions now and then." He drew a sip through the long straw.

"Then I was redefined as vertically challenged. It became incorrect to gawk at me. Receipts were way down. I had to be flexible and think about changing careers myself." The midget shrugged and took another sip.

"That's what got me into this line of work. It's not so bad. The contortionist here used to be a lawyer. It wasn't such a big change for him." Everyone chuckled.

"Now let's see if we can figure out where you fit in the corporate food chain," said the midget.

"Deadwood City."

"High-rise outhouse."

"Calculates door points."

"Hmm," said the midget, scratching his cheek. "The thin man thinks you work in Human Resources, calculating the salary point at which an employee will say 'screw it' and head for the door, then recommending a salary two percent above that level. However, I feel you are not oily and creepy enough to work in Human Resources. I feel you calculate the prices of things that your company buys. Are you head of the purchasing department?"

Dad's jaw dropped open.

"Ah, it's been a very good day for me today," said the midget, looking pleased. "For ten dollars more, I will tell you the future of purchasing."

Dad swallowed and nodded affirmatively.

"Mixed. Failing companies will keep it centralized; successful companies will empower the front line troops. You will have to learn something else besides mere haggling to survive. Rapid change, my friend. Rapid change. Please leave twenty dollars with the thin man. Oh, and your son would make an exceptionally well-qualified cab driver."

Dad got up and gave the thin man twenty dollars. It was snatched. Brent and Audey followed him out to the car.

Audey fell asleep on the way home. Dad didn't say too much. Brent was a little dazed. The food and the rides were great, but the career estimator was spooky. Still, he wasn't too worried. He was headed for college in a couple of weeks. When he had his PhD in particle physics, he would be able to pretty much pick and choose whatever job he wanted. He was smart. That job stuff didn't apply to him.

Death Looked Down

This is my first novelette, penned in March of 1994. The genesis was a paragraph about global warming in Vital Signs 1993 *that reminded me of an image that I had tucked away in my head thirteen years earlier. That image, of priests living along a dry, but still sacred, riverbed in Calcutta, was from the April-June 1962 issue of* Man in India *I had read for a graduate seminar. Other images started popping into my head, so I decided to make a story of them. I spent a few months going through the seminar materials, made an honest-to-God outline—this story is four times longer than my previous longest—then sat down to write. The title is purloined from Kipling.*

Dawn Albright was kind enough to include it in her New Altars *anthology, so this is the story that made me a published author. Excelsior!*

Reverend Sir turned his head and looked at the crocodile. The crocodile looked back at him. Reverend Sir shook his head very slightly back and forth. The crocodile swam away.

Reverend Sir turned his head back again and looked at the man sitting before him. The man had earlier been pacing back and forth; gesturing wildly, yelling and swearing in English. Now he was slumped back in his chair. His left hand was resting in midair a foot above his emaciated brown belly. His right hand grasped an imaginary clicker. He kept pressing it with his thumb, flicking through channel after channel with a dull look on his face. One channel grabbed his attention and he leapt to his feet.

"Goddamn that asshole Dan Rather! That bleeding heart liberal prick! Those food stamp fuckers are hungry and homeless because they don't have the balls to pull themselves up by their bootstraps the way I did. GodDAMN him!" The man started pacing again, his fists balled up and resting six inches on either side of his protruding hip bones. Every time he walked in front of the chair, he would reach down into an imaginary bag of potato chips and stuff them into his mouth.

Reverend Sir looked at the other two men on the platform. They were quite baffled and looked at Reverend Sir imploringly. Mr. Bose spoke English, but was having a hard time with the man's American accent. Mr. Sen, the man's older brother, spoke only Bengali. Since the man himself also spoke only Bengali, they had put him in a boat and rowed all night back to Calcutta to bring him to Reverend Sir. He would surely know what to do.

"As one sows, so shall one reap," said Reverend Sir, in Bengali. "It is the law of karma."

"Ah, karma," said Mr. Bose and Mr. Sen together and knowingly. What else could it be? A previous life was coming back to the surface.

Reverend Sir recited a long mantra, then stepped up to the man and smacked him hard on the face, knocking him down. "Come back! Come back!" he shouted.

The man looked up glassy eyed at Reverend Sir, then at the other two. He moaned and muttered something to himself. His head drooped down.

"Thank you, Reverend Sir," said Mr. Sen. "Please take these as a small token." He handed Reverend Sir a large bundle of food wrapped in a banana leaf and tied with string. Mr. Bose handed him some drinking coconuts and bottles of soda.

"You would rather not be coming with us?" asked Mr. Sen. "Surely you have stayed here as long as anyone could expect. All the other holy men have left. The goddess will not be angry."

Reverend Sir stood up straight and tall and paused a moment. His sacred thread looped over one shoulder. A simple cotton dhoti was wrapped around his waist. His quiet brown eyes surveyed the landscape of dingy, decaying buildings, half submerged by the monsoon floods. He had been asked this question many times before. Yet he still could not say why he felt he shouldn't leave.

"No, you two go and take this poor fellow with you. Remember: as one acts, so one becomes. That is karma. That is what will determine the nature of our new lives."

They all said their namashkars. The man was lifted down into the boat. The two men pushed off from the platform and rowed away.

Reverend Sir carried the food and drink into the small thatched hut he had built for himself, stepping directly on the face of the greatest Bengali cinema star of all time. When his temple had first flooded, Reverend Sir had asked the neighborhood boys to scavenge some wood for him to build a platform on the temple's roof. They came gleefully back with an abandoned cinema billboard. In the middle was this fool cinema star; two rows of white teeth and oversized sunglasses. His fist was raised to the sky and one foot was crushing a globe beneath it. Bengal triumphant! But now the paint was wearing away from the rain, the heat and Reverend Sir's footsteps.

It is a sign of the times, these past lives coming to the surface, thought Reverend Sir as he stowed his food. Certainly a great tragedy has befallen mankind. Perhaps, even, we are coming to the end of this cycle of existence. Perhaps, too, the panic from this plane of existence has spread to other ones and the orderly transmigration of souls has become disrupted. It was hard to say. Reverend Sir often pondered these types of questions, but he always found it difficult to come to firm conclusions. Every school of thought said something different. He liked to keep an open mind.

He had finally decided some months ago that speculation alone would be inadequate to answer these types of questions. His older brother, whom everyone referred to by his initials, N. K., was a brilliant civil engineer. They used to debate with each other about everything under the sun. N. K.'s trump card was always empirical proof. Where was Reverend Sir's empirical proof? What kind of proof was quoting dusty old Sanskrit tomes? Were the Vedas based on a standard model of the Big Bang, or a nonstandard model?

Reverend Sir did the best he could in these debates, but the two brothers were so different. Reverend Sir liked to slowly ponder things, while N. K. was like a computer—his tongue flicking out the answers, flick, flick, flick. Now that the last of those requiring his help had departed, Reverend Sir was ready to try to find some clues to his situation.

A wandering yogi had once passed through his temple and had offered instruction in reliving past lives in return for food and a place to sleep. Reverend Sir was not too interested in this knowledge at the time and would've given the yogi food and shelter anyway. But the yogi—his eyes so clear and deep beneath his matted locks—had a persuasive way about him. So Reverend Sir learned the technique, but did not practice it at the time.

Now he felt it was time. He had done the preparatory exercises and meditations. According to the yogi, what life one returned to was controlled by concentrating on when that life happened. Reverend Sir—not wanting to get stuck in some life millions of lifetimes ago—decided to go back one century on his first attempt.

He walked out of his hut and sat in the center of the platform, square on the cinema star's chest. He commenced the final phase.

Very gradually he began to feel light and buoyant. Then he started to rise in the air. He commanded that it become bright and sunny, and it became so. As he rose, Calcutta shimmered up out of the flood waters and laid itself out for him.

First, directly beneath him, he saw his temple along the Adiganga, the original bed of the river Ganga. To his left were the Kidderpore Docks, with some merchantmen tucked safely away from the Hooghly river's treacherous currents. As he rose higher, he gazed upon the Maidan, Calcutta's Central Park. It was a giant green lung, fully two square miles in size, and studded with treasures: the Victoria Memorial, Birla Planetarium, Fort William, the Ochterlony Monument. His eyes followed Chowringhee—Calcutta's main road, running along the east edge of the Maidan—northward toward the original Howrah Bridge. He could even spot Howrah Station way across the Hooghly!

Now he started to descend. He tried to avoid panicking as he came down faster and faster. He landed with a thump on the sidewalk of Chowringhee.

"O young learned gentlemen, you must be confusing me with someone else!" cried Reverend Sir, desperately.

"O no, old ignorant fool! You are exactly the one we want," replied the leader of the group of students.

"But I am just a simple priest, tending a small temple. Politics is not for me," said Reverend Sir.

"You are delivering opium to the masses. They cannot develop proper consciousness while they are being fed drivel. We have initiated a properly disciplined program of militant mass action. The battle has been joined according to the materialist principles of class conflict. Your kind is part of the old society. You will be gheraoed until you agree to learn and disseminate proper Marxism. Or until you die," said the student leader.

Reverend Sir peered into the young man's face. He wasn't bluffing. Nor did he have a sense of humor. Reverend Sir didn't really understand all of the jargon the student was shoving at him, but he did realize that he was a man of the spirit and not a materialist. The businessmen that came to worship at his temple sometimes spoke nervously about gheraos. The only thing to do was to wait and hope the police showed up.

So Reverend Sir sat down on the sidewalk, surrounded by these university students. He could hear the crash and roar of Calcutta— the blowing horns of taxis, the calls of street vendors, the clanking bells of rickshaws—beyond the students, but he was totally cut off. It was a typical day in April: 106 degrees, 98% humidity. Reverend

Sir sat exposed to the sun; the students had umbrellas for shade. He tried not to faint.

Gheraos were one of the most punishing and effective weapons in the arsenal of Bengali politics. The target—an employer, a professor, a judge—would suddenly find himself surrounded by a band of men. They wouldn't touch him, but if he tried to leave he would be beaten to death. More dastardly still was when the men relieved each other on a shift system, while the victim dehydrated in the noonday sun. Such was the situation Reverend Sir found himself in as he waited for the police to show up.

If and when they showed up. Gheraos had become so common—and the power of the Communist Party of India (Marxist) so strong—that the police often showed up very late. It was part of the madness enveloping this great city. There were riots almost every day; some small, some covering large swaths of the city. Bombs were placed and businesses shattered. Fires sprung up and God was to be thanked if there was water pressure that day for the hoses. Political murders were a common occurrence. And this was only the political violence! If religion became involved, the whole metropolis went insane with hate and revenge.

"Clear the sidewalks! Do not congregate! Be on your way!" Reverend Sir raised his head as he heard these words coming from beyond the circle of students. One of the students came forward and gave him a few kicks. Then they all ran off.

A small platoon of police was coming down the sidewalk, swinging their bamboo staves. They gave the students a brief chase. A pious shopkeeper darted out of his shop and gave Reverend Sir a glass of water. He gulped it down. The shopkeeper disappeared quickly, lest he be marked for reprisals.

"Head straight home, Sir. Today is not a good day for holy men to be about in this part of town," said the platoon leader. Reverend Sir thanked him and started walking south on Chowringhee as quickly as he could. At every intersection were two policemen watching for terrorists. Standing back to back, their Enfield rifles were loaded and pointed directly into oncoming traffic.

Reverend Sir began to breathe easier as he returned to his own neighborhood. He wound his way through the narrow streets and alleys between the small factories and workshops that had grown up around his temple. Normally, he was somewhat peeved at these houses of commerce occupying sacred land on the banks of the Adi-ganga, pressing so close to his temple. So what if the Ganga had shifted its course and this river bed was mostly dry now? It was still sacred. The Hooghly wasn't sacred. Why couldn't they conduct business over there? But after today's ghastly events, he found their familiar presence reassuring. Besides, once a month these same businessmen came to his temple and laid their ledgers at the feet of the goddess. They received her blessing and always left a donation. So it would be churlish to bite the hand that fed him. It was no longer like the old days, when his temple was supported out of virtue alone. People even came when registering a vehicle or renewing a driver's license. Students also came for the blessing of the goddess at examination time. Who was he to deny them peace of mind? What did those gheraoers know about the value of these things? Did they want drivers plying Calcutta's horribly congested streets without proper self-confidence?

Reverend Sir turned the corner and walked up the lane to his temple. The barred doors of the sanctum sanctorum containing the goddess were closed until the evening's worship, but he mentally prostrated himself to her in thanksgiving for his safe return. He walked around back to his small living quarters. His young assistant was sitting on the step, reading *The Statesman* and drinking a cup of tea. He popped up when Reverend Sir came into view.

"Reverend Sir! You are very late. Did everything go well? I made sure the goddess was resting comfortably for the afternoon break."

"Please make me some tea. Extra large and extra sweet. Also some small tidbit," said Reverend Sir.

After seating himself, he related the day's events to his assistant, who was horrified and sympathetic, making tsk tsking sounds throughout. When he had finished the tale (already somewhat embellished even on this first telling) the two of them sat there behind the temple in the early evening, sharing the silence.

The assistant broke it first. "Perhaps when you retire, you should stay with your relatives inland in Burdwan? I am not at all optimistic about this city. How can such a thing be such a commonplace? It is the overcrowding—that is what makes people's tempers so hot. An entire family will rent out just the space underneath a staircase in the old houses from British days. Professorji said the population of Calcutta is 102,000 per square mile, while that of New York City is only 27,000, and yet they have many skyscrapers and we have none. And it is getting worse. Today's paper said two thousand refugees a day are arriving in the city from East Pakistan. If war breaks out, that number will surely increase." And so the assistant rattled on for some while, spouting statistics like a fountain on the Maidan.

Reverend Sir wasn't sure if this young man was really suitable to be a priest. A priest's mind should turn inward to itself and not outward to the experiential world. Why such an interest in the details of society? Our lives are like those of mosquitoes, compared to those in the higher planes. Reverend Sir blamed it on Professorji, a truly absurd figure if there ever was one. One day, Reverend Sir came out of the temple to find his assistant talking to a very pale man wearing leather boots that reached from his toes to his waist. Covered his entire legs! In the hot season, no less. After he had left, his assistant said he was an American and something called a social scientist and wore the boots to guard against snake bites. Furthermore, his assistant was now employed part time as an "informant." Reverend Sir was very skeptical about this arrangement, and told his assistant not to inform the pale man about the secrets of the goddess, nor to detail the contributions they received. The assistant sincerely vowed not to do so. But from that day on, his Bengali became ever more infested with English words like "kinship," "census data" and the completely incomprehensible "correlation coefficient."

Reverend Sir interjected, "Burdwan is not for me. I must stay with the goddess. Now I am going inside to take a nap. I am not feeling completely myself today."

Reverend Sir lay splayed out on the platform, his mouth open and facing skyward. Stars began struggling to glow through the sticky air. A century was a long time to sleep. He opened his eyes and then closed them. What was he doing outside? Then it flooded back into him. He moaned and rolled over on his side. He had helped so many people back from experiencing their past lives, yet he did not know until now just how wrenching it was. Perhaps he should have been gentler and more sympathetic to them. Reverend Sir got up and went into his hut and found one of the bottles. Then he popped open the Soma Cola and sat in the doorway to watch the moon rise.

He was quite baffled by what he had just gone through. Reverend Sir had not imagined that samsara, the wheel of birth and death, operated like this. He had thought it possible that he may have been very rich or very poor; maybe a European or an African or a Japanese; maybe a woman, even; maybe even not a human at all, but rather anything from a microorganism to a deity in the highest level of heaven. But it never occurred to him that he would be himself. In the constant passage of the soul from one body to another, why would the soul come back to what was, in a way, the same body? He was not exactly the Dalai Lama, after all.

Reverend Sir drained the bottle and set it down. He got up to get N. K.'s picture. He always smiled a bit when he looked at it. It was N. K.'s wedding photo. And how was the ultrarational civil engineer dressed? In fine silk garments, all traditionally styled. The print itself even had a simulated sepia tone. Then he recalled his brother's fate, and his eyes moistened. It was usually like that: first a slight smile, then a small tear.

Reverend Sir remembered well the day N. K. was admitted to the Eastern India Civil Engineering Authority. Those men and women were the heroes of the nation. And no one looked up to them more than N. K. When he joined, he had found his destiny. Soon he became one of their most brilliant stars. He threw himself into his work and would talk of nothing else. Reverend Sir would listen with admiration, and some thankfulness, that he was no longer debating that computer-like mind.

According to N. K., global warming was a serious problem that, with courage and commitment, could be handled—but at a high cost, and with little margin for error. The initial projections made in the late 20th century—a seven-inch rise in the sea level by 2030, a fourteen-inch rise by 2060—turned out to be fairly accurate. When Reverend Sir heard these numbers, they didn't sound so bad to him. What was one more foot of water?

N. K. admitted that Calcutta was some 25 feet above sea level and 80 miles or so distant from the Bay of Bengal. The problem was that the tidal range was 22 feet, and the water table always remained close to the surface—or even came above it during the monsoon floods. The soil of Calcutta, surrounded by swamps since its founding, was waterlogged and jellylike even before the warming began. Now it was even soggier. Floods…deforestation in the Himalayas… increased soil salinity…thermal expansion of ocean waters. Mutual negative reinforcement, or something like that, N. K. called it. Tidal bores came rushing up the Hooghly most days of the year. The worst cyclones in recorded history began to hit with ghastly regularity. Reverend Sir found one fact especially distasteful: water lines and sewer lines had been installed side by side. When pipes broke, the two fluids mixed.

The temperature, too, rose higher as the 21st century progressed. Although the average global temperature rose only a few degrees, the tropics were disproportionately affected. And when a heat wave came…well, Calcutta had days above 110 degrees before the warming. Now it never went below 100 in the hot season, even at night. A midday temperature of 130 was no longer uncommon. Not even mad dogs went about in that. One unforeseen effect was that the tar in roads would liquefy and drain away, so it became difficult to keep roads paved. Buildings also decayed rapidly. The whole city looked filthier and dingier than ever.

It was a thoroughly demoralizing situation. Yet somehow, Calcutta—indeed, all of India; the whole world—rallied. The Ford Foundation sparked the World Bank. The IMF followed the Bank. The UN weighed in, not wanting to be left behind. Other deltaic cities—New Orleans and Rotterdam, Shanghai and El Iskandaria, Guangzhou and Yangon, Bangkok and New Saigon—realized they were in the same boat and initiated DeltaNet to share strategies and tactics. Miracle of miracles, the governments in Calcutta and Delhi even ceased their endless bickering to form the Eastern India Civil Engineering Authority. A vast and elaborate scheme of dams and dikes, spillways and canals, was developed to protect all of eastern India from the rising waters. Bureaucracy was shoved aside to get the mud flying. It was inspiring and heroic. It was the project of the age, like America's long-ago effort to put a man on the moon. It was N. K.'s calling in life, and he threw himself into it. It would be tough, but it could be done.

Then, quite suddenly and without warning, global warming went nonlinear.

Reverend Sir got up and gently put the picture of his brother back in its place. Then he said good night to the goddess, sleeping in her watery abode beneath him, and crawled into bed. Thankfully, he slept without dreaming.

When Reverend Sir woke up late the next morning, the rain was coming down solidly. It splattered all over the cinema star, wearing him away a bit more. His hut was still not leaking and he was very happy about that. He turned on his little cook stove to make some breakfast. Some tea would also do quite nicely.

He still wasn't sure what to make of yesterday's experience. It seemed as real as anything he had ever undergone. He just didn't know how to interpret it. Reverend Sir decided to try again after breakfast. He thought he would go back two centuries this time.

Reverend Sir sat on the floor in padmasana, the lotus position, and wrapped his left arm around the center pole of his hut. He was afraid of thrashing around during his experience and didn't want to damage anything or find his way outside. He calmed his mind and began the procedure.

That delicious buoyancy returned. He rose right through the roof and high into the sky. Reverend Sir willed the rain to stop falling, the clouds to part, the sun to burst forth and send golden rays over all of creation. And it did. Calcutta glistened and shone like a silvery fish leaping out of dark water. Its exuberance exploded like a million verses of poetry. It dazzled the universe with its joy and sparkle. So full of life!

Reverend Sir felt himself starting to descend and tried to stay calm. He was looking back up at the sun, longing for its radiance, not watching where he was coming down. He landed hard in the north-west corner of the Maidan, on Strand Road along the Hooghly.

Reverend Sir (as he was later to be known) cursed himself for his rashness. He was sure he was being followed. He quickened his step a bit more and looked over his shoulder into the dark night for the thousandth time. Still no one. What a fool he was! The kind priest at the last pilgrims' hostel had warned him that thugs roamed freely at night. The other pilgrims had murmured agreement. One traveler said that Kali needed to be sacrificed to every day. Goats were good. Buffaloes were better. Humans were best. The thugs would offer a silver coin to Kali for her blessing, then knot it in the end of a strangling cloth to give them a better grip. Another man said thugs would throw children to the sharks in the Hooghly. A third volunteered that, besides, the weather did not look good. Reverend Sir replied, with the bravado of the young, that he was anxious to return to his parents' house in 24 Parganas District. Furthermore, he was young and strong and would do it by skipping every other hostel along the pilgrimage route, walking twice the usual daily distance. What a fool!

Reverend Sir kept peeking over at the Hooghly as he hurried. He could see little. There didn't seem to be any sacrifices or shark feasts in progress. He looked to his left and saw the formidable mass of Fort William. The big guns lurking inside enjoyed a clear field of fire, ready for insurrection. Now he feared that a British patrol might issue forth from its gates and happen upon him. Every native knew that there were two standards of justice in Bengal. Reverend Sir also knew that he didn't have the money to purchase the better of the two. He quickly looked behind him for the thousandth and first time. Still no one. The very desertion of the place was ominous. He kept walking.

A road running diagonally through the Maidan intersected the Strand. He paused briefly. If he continued on the Strand, he would wind up near the Kidderpore Docks, which were sure to be quite deserted. If he took the diagonal, he would cross the Maidan and could then walk south on Chowringhee. Reverend Sir chose the latter.

The wind began gusting as he scurried across the Maidan. Surely, someone could sneak up on him now without being heard, he thought. He began to alternate walking forwards with walking backwards. Every so often there was a street lamp containing a flickering coconut oil flame. The wind blew one of these out as he was passing underneath and it made him jump. He looked up and saw that the sky was beginning to redden. He didn't like the looks of it at all. It shouldn't be getting brighter—twilight had long since gone.

Reverend Sir made it to Chowringhee and headed south. Those few people still out were scurrying home. A rickshaw wallah ran by, hauling a fat rich woman. Her brocaded silk sari was flapping in the wind; his bare feet made little noise. A block later, four bearers struggled with a palanquin in the wind. The two Europeans inside yelled at them to keep it level, all the while lolling about with their cigars and bottles of whiskey.

Reverend Sir was beginning to succumb to panic. The wind was quickly turning into a gale, and rain was starting to whip into him. The sky was on fire and that was terrifying. He forgot all about thugs—he was out walking in a cyclone now.

He kept walking as best he could. He was knocked down flat three times. He saw what looked like a hostel up ahead. Even if it wasn't, he had to stop and take shelter. Reverend Sir staggered up the steps and went inside the porch. He wrapped his left arm around a pillar and collapsed from exhaustion. He fell asleep like that. The winds howled through, but he was dry.

"Ah, the young sir has awakened," said a voice.

Reverend Sir blinked and raised his head slightly. He blinked again and looked in the direction of the voice. A half dozen feet away sat a middle-aged man. His hair was oiled and combed straight back, away from his black-framed glasses. He was very clean shaven, almost dapper looking.

"I see you are returning to the land of the living after all. Very good," said the man. "I tried to pry you away from that column early this morning. But you were hanging on as if your life depended on it, as perhaps indeed it was. That was quite a storm we had last night. Do you take tea?"

Reverend Sir nodded that he did. The man poured him a small cup, then continued, "You were quite fortunate to find this place. Many buildings were damaged, but this temple was built to last."

"This is a temple?" asked Reverend Sir.

"Oh yes. To the goddess. She gathered you into her last night. I am but her humble and obedient servant. All this means nothing to me," he said, waving his arm vaguely about. "I enjoy the use of it, but I am not attached to it."

Reverend Sir sipped at his tea and looked about him. He believed he recognized this neighborhood from his journey north. That was the Adiganga over there. This was a pleasant place—close to the city, but not swallowed up by it. A few people were out and about, assessing the damage and what they would do about it.

"Is your home nearby?" asked the man.

"No, I am returning to my parents' house in 24 Parganas. I went to see the great Ramakrishna at Dakshineswar. I was caught in the storm between hostels."

"Ah, a religious young man," said the man, giving Reverend Sir a very penetrating, sideways look. "Very good. Very good. Yes, Ramakrishna is certainly justly renowned. I must say, though, that I myself follow the path of knowledge, rather than the path of devotion."

A young boy came up and gave the man a copy of *The Englishman,* receiving a coin in exchange. He hurried off.

"Do you read English?" asked Reverend Sir, his eyes widening.

"Oh yes. And Bengali. And Sanskrit. Even a small bit of Urdu and Persian. Mine is the path of knowledge," he said, looking down his nose at the paper. "Only two pages long today. I am surprised they got it out at all. Mostly about the weather . . . 146 mile per hour winds, with a storm surge measuring twenty feet at the coast . . . oh my goodness . . . out of 195 ships in port, 36 were sunk and a further 97 were badly damaged, many thrown high and dry . . . the loss of human life not even estimated at this time." He continued scanning the paper, his glance darting about its surface, occasionally making small noises in his throat. When he had satisfied himself that he had learned everything there was to be learned from it, he folded it neatly under his arm and stood up.

"You must be very hungry, young sir. You are my guest. There will be few worshipers today. Stay with me for lunch and perhaps a few days while the damage is cleared. Then you can resume your journey. I will show you the goddess that saved you, then see to the preparations."

The man led him inside and opened the doors to the sanctum sanctorum. A few oil lamps were already burning, casting a dull yellow glow. He beheld the form of the goddess. It was a beautiful image, though certainly not as awe inspiring as the one he saw in Dakshineswar. But he didn't recognize it.

"Which goddess is this?" he asked.

"This is the primeval goddess herself; the pure undifferentiated feminine. This form is actually quite rare," said the man.

Something inside Reverend Sir melted. A crazy fantasy that he should devote his life to serving this goddess filled his head. He stood transfixed—for how long, he did not know. Finally, he closed the doors and began looking around the temple. It was neither large and ostentatious, nor small and plain. Whoever designed it had a superior sense of proportion and sound judgment about ornamentation. It felt just right to him. Around back was a small room. There he found the man sitting on the floor behind one of two banana leaves, waiting for him.

"Reading English is a very important thing, young sir. We are sitting, after all, but a stone's throw away from the second city of the British Empire. The Viceroy is second only to the Sovereign herself;

above even the Prime Minister in the opinion of many. The administration of such a vast dominion requires many trained personnel. We should have a part in it."

He wasn't entirely sure he was hearing this man correctly. He didn't seem to mind the British, as long as he could share in the spoils.

"But surely the British have neglected everything but the pursuit of money," he ventured.

The man's hand fell to his leaf. "You are not one of those young hotheads, are you? Those Sepoys were rascals, one and all. Calcutta has become a city of palaces. It used to take many weeks to travel even as far as Banaras. Now one can take the Grand Trunk Road all the way to Peshawar. Walk along the Hooghly. Ships that sail all around the world have their keels laid in Kidderpore. You will see the jute mills, producing gunny sacks and carpet backing to be used throughout the Empire. This is the beginning of industrialization. And don't think we don't influence them. Throughout England, people speak of bungalows. And what are they? Nothing but 'Bengal houses.'"

Reverend Sir listened quietly that day, that first day in his temple. The man went on for some time about the glories of Calcutta, even as the first putrid whiffs from the bloating human and animal corpses began to waft through the temple. Great schools of hilsa fish were left stranded on land, and those began to rot, too. Dead crows lay everywhere. There was garbage floating in the low soggy areas surrounding the city. Cholera and other diseases cheerily availed themselves of the Grand Trunk Road and spread through north and east India for some months after the cyclone. But he just dreamed of the goddess.

He stayed on and made himself indispensable to that odd, worldly priest. Only once did Reverend Sir make it down to his parents' house; to ask for their permission to take up his new career. For when the miscast priest was offered a choice position at Calcutta University—which he readily accepted—Reverend Sir assumed the position that was rightfully his.

The rain was still falling when Reverend Sir slowly remembered who he was and when he was. The disorientation was worse than the first time. His left arm was still wrapped around the center pole, and it was stiff beyond feeling. He loosened it with his right arm, then reached up to his table to look at his clock. It was still the same day! In his first experience, there seemed to be roughly a one-to-one correspondence between real time and past life time. But now he remembered many years as a young man during the Raj. He also still remembered his more recent life as the old man caught in the gherao. Three lives lived in him now, all linked to this temple. His head felt overstuffed. He decided to take a break from reliving past lives until he could regain some sense of normalcy.

So he spent several days idling in his hut when it was raining; going out on his platform when it wasn't. He saw no one now—not in boats, not even in planes. The pilots were no doubt worried about mechanical failure. If they went down, who would rescue them? No one. He read his sacred books and wondered how and why this all could happen. He worked his way through the remaining food at a steady pace. The drinking coconuts were a double treat: first one drinks them, then one slurps up the tender meat. Mostly, he tried to survive the heat and humidity while resting for his third stab at the past.

On one of those days, he looked at N. K.'s picture again and broke down weeping. Not so much for N. K. that time, as for the cruel way fate turned possible victory into tragedy. Even now, he had difficulty comprehending the scope of it.

He first suspected something was wrong from a change in N. K.'s demeanor. N. K. was always optimistic about the challenge, always able to lay out the advantages and disadvantages of this or that approach, able to recalculate and make adjustments, able to change his tactics to serve his strategy. But when the warming started to deviate from projections, N. K. was no longer able to make the numbers add up, no matter how many times he tried, no matter how many allowances he made, no matter what. It showed on his face and in the sag of his shoulders. And in this day and age, secrets of this magnitude cannot be kept secret for long.

Not surprisingly, the first reaction of the public to the news was denial. If everyone pitched in and just worked harder, it was said, the tide could literally be turned. A historian wrote a letter to the editor informing the public that the jute mills of Bengal supplied eight million sandbags a month to the lads on the Western Front in World War I. The Calcutta Chamber of Commerce promptly launched a campaign to refit and reopen some of the old mills, closed decades ago due to competition from synthetics. The grimy, red-brick buildings began once again to produce sandbags by the millions. But a bag full of quicksand thrown into a pool of quicksand is not too effective. The effort was dropped very quietly, so as not to damage morale.

The first Durga Puja held after it was generally known that things were going badly was the most splendid in living memory. Glittering and festive displays—dubbed religious Rose Bowl floats by one American journalist—were erected throughout the city, bringing traffic to a standstill for days. So many prayers were said that there arose a general expectation that Durga herself would incarnate and save the city. Many people sat awake at night, looking skyward, so as not to miss that auspicious event. The Puja was even optimistically extended for several days. No reliable sightings were confirmed.

The situation over the border in Bangladesh was getting truly desperate. The hundred million and more landless peasants were trying to live on islands of silt, but these kept getting washed away. When one's island began to wash away, one had no choice but to invade another island—which was always already occupied and ready to be defended to the death. The brutality and savagery of these hand-to-hand battles was total. After a while, Bangladesh became too dangerous for journalists to cover. So it tended to slip out of one's mind, when one had so many of one's own problems closer at hand. Some suspected the Indian Armed Forces had stepped up their border patrols, since the flow of refugees never became very heavy. But this was never reported anywhere. Most people, when and if they thought about it, lamely hoped for the best; that the Bangladeshis were managing to cope on their own.

Countless people in Calcutta were having trouble coping themselves. Suicide became very common. The preferred method was jumping off one of the bridges crossing the Hooghly. These leapers—as they came to be known—were so numerous, that ships plying the river erected tent-shaped scaffolding and nets over their decks to deflect the leapers into the water. Indeed, it became so bad that an ordinance was passed, requesting leapers to restrict themselves to certain sections of the original Howrah Bridge, thereby removing the danger to navigation. Amazingly, there was enough civic spirit left in the leapers for them to queue up at the entrance to the bridge, calmly waiting their turn. A minor uproar ensued when neighborhood toughs began to extort money from the leapers, in return for letting them on the bridge. Even more grisly was that the toughs also made money by catching and selling the sharks and crocodiles that had grown fat on the leapers.

But those toughs were just small bit actors. Calcutta was about extracting money from the day it was founded until the last final instant. If one listened closely, one could hear the sound of capital rushing out of the city. Profiteering in misery became rampant as everyone tried to turn one last rupee. A small item in the newspaper noted without comment that prostitution was now the most widely practiced occupation. Food hoarding became common and bribes could always be paid to keep one's hoard intact. Even better was to start a panic by spreading rumors of food hoarding, thereby increasing the value of your stores. Medicine was especially valuable as malaria and cholera, dysentery and typhus, influenza and even the plague became chronic. All were fed by the malnutrition caused by both the real, and the manufactured, shortages of food.

And of course, across the Hooghly in Howrah, Calcutta's Bronx, everything was much worse.

The public's mood darkened noticeably when the subway had to be abandoned due to water saturation, its white marble thoroughly stained. It had been a source of pride since its construction in the late 20th century. Built by Indians themselves, it ran on schedule down to the half minute. Also discouraging was when the effort to keep roads paved was abandoned.

It was decided that perhaps a massive hunger strike in the Gandhian tradition would prick the world's conscience and bring outside aid. Thousands came to the Maidan to participate. By this time, however, air traffic flowing in and out of Dum Dum airport had become increasingly sporadic. Foreign news crews were reluctant to provide coverage. So local news teams did the best they could and beamed it out. Many of the strikers fasted to their deaths. Moving speeches were made across the globe, but the rest of the world was also having problems coping with the warming.

When the hunger strike yielded no results, a massive rally was held on the Maidan. Two million people converged to display their anger. A dozen different flavors of communists arrived, marching in disciplined columns twenty abreast, waving bright red banners. Followers of Netaji, the Bengali nationalist hero from World War II, arrived in strength. They carried a large empty sedan chair, just in case Netaji should choose this moment to return and lead them to victory. Each member of the Tagore family had a small but vocal following, as did Mother Theresa. The Gandhians were somewhat reduced in number, due to the poor results of the hunger strike. It was a glorious rally, the speakers' amplified voices billowing across the city in great waves of rising and falling Bengali rhetoric. Fantasies of power were spun and cast, spun and cast.

But after several hours in the heat, tempers grew short. When one speaker's 17-point action program contradicted an earlier speaker's 11-point plan of action, far back in the crowd a Netaji supporter taunted a member of the Revolutionary Socialist Party. That man answered with a gun. The Netaji supporters pulled out their guns and began firing. The crowd of two million turned into a mob of two million.

And then, Calcutta was barely heard from for three days.

One would not think it possible, in this day of advanced communications, for a city to cut itself off so completely, but Calcutta did. There was not a premeditated plan to choke the roads with wrecks, to burn the rail stations, to swarm upon the planes until the wings collapsed, to plunge the city into darkness. That was simply the byproduct. When that crowd became a mob, the whole city became a mob. Centuries of frustration and desperation at last erupted. People began to kill each other with their bare hands, if nothing else was available. Portable communication devices still worked, but their owners were too busy killing, or being killed, to use them. The rich and the poor had always lived side by side—and now the poor had nothing to lose. Birla Park, home of the Birlas, Marwari businessmen from Rajasthan and India's wealthiest family, was sacked. When the slum dwellers came upon the ice skating rink within, still operating, they literally did not know, could not comprehend, what they were looking at. The horrors of political and religious violence in the 20th century were but the mildest of precursors. At the beginning of the rally, the metropolitan area had sixteen million inhabitants. Three days later, but eight million.

N. K. was in Delhi at the time of the riot, and so was safe. Reverend Sir still wondered how he himself had survived. Two of the days were spent locked in the sanctum sanctorum with the goddess. He could hear the shouts and fighting outside. On the last day, he helped put out fires in the neighborhood.

Reverend Sir remembered all these things and they weighed heavily upon him. He checked his stores and decided it was time to go back to an earlier life—three centuries back. The rains were falling again, so he decided to stay inside this time as well. He was more confident about controlling himself during the experience, so he decided to spare his arm and sit in the small open space. He began the procedure.

It was slower to come this time, but it came. Reverend Sir began to feel light. And he began to feel happy as well. He started rising up, right through the roof of the hut. The rains ceased at his merest thought that they should do so. Calcutta began to glow with the energy of a giant chakra. The chakra began to spin and the city pulsed beneath it. Centrifugal force blew the chakra away, leaving Calcutta immaculate and pure. He was high above it now. He was stationary, not yet falling. "Why is the city so perfect when I rise above it this way?" he wondered. "Is this how it will be reborn in its next life, in the coming age?" He started falling now, straight down onto the steps of his own temple. He landed flat on his back, hard.

Reverend Sir lay dying. He was very old, very sick and very hungry. He was lying on a cot placed on the porch of the temple. It was too hot to stay inside. He opened his eyes and looked for the boy. He didn't see him. Reverend Sir thought the boy was there a moment ago, but he wasn't sure.

Reverend Sir had been passing in and out of delirium for days now. Last night was the longest night of his life. Every minute was an hour; every hour, a century. His liver and pancreas were swollen and hard. Fever would pour through his body, making him sweat suddenly from every pore. Then a chill would pass through, and his sweat would feel like ice water. He would call out for the boy—or intended to call out, thought he called out—and the boy would tap his stick on the porch to let Reverend Sir know he was still there, still watching out for him.

Reverend Sir didn't like the way his body smelled—like a carcass, ripe for the taking. Jackals were getting bolder each night in their search for dead bodies. Sometimes they did not wait for the body to be completely dead. As long as it could not fight back, that was enough. Even domesticated dogs would do this, they were so hungry. (Although fortunately there were few of these around, since so many had already been eaten. As were rats. And snails.) Crows would also land on one and pluck away. Even leopards and tigers were stalking again at night, just like in his childhood. That's why he hired the boy, to look after him.

"Boy! Boy!" he tried to bellow out, but it was barely a whisper. Reverend Sir couldn't remember his name. The boy had been abandoned to his fate when he came begging to Reverend Sir's temple. Dharma was collapsing throughout the land. Children and babies were being abandoned and sold. The very old and the sick were not receiving proper care. Widows were being asked by their families to leave and make do on their own. Prostitution for a handful of rice was common. Families were selling everything they owned for food.

Since Reverend Sir himself had just been left to his own fate, he thought that he and the boy could help each other. He had already been feeling ill and weak at that point. The memory of his relatives leaving him drove him mad with anger.

"Here I am, Reverend Sir. Here is today's rice for you," said the boy. The cup held three spoonfuls. The boy fed him the three spoonfuls. Reverend Sir chewed them very slowly, savoring every grain.

The boy, being smaller, then slowly ate two spoonfuls from his cup. They sat looking at each other when they finished. One could study the anatomy of the entire human skeleton, just by observing this boy. Yet somehow the boy smiled, glad to have two spoonfuls of rice, glad no one tried to steal it out of his hands.

Who is responsible for this? Reverend Sir wondered. What god or goddess is punishing us, and why? What are we being punished for? Were vows broken? Was some divine artifact stolen? Or is man himself responsible for this? Is it the fault of those Englishmen in the East India Company? He had heard stories of what it was like to work on their indigo plantations. Little more than slavery. But at least they had the good sense to stretch a chain across the Hooghly to stop the pirates from raiding at will. Is it due to malfeasance by the Nawab in Murshidabad? One of his worshipers had an uncle in Murshidabad that was accused of stealing. The Nawab's men stitched him up in a pair of baggy pants, then threw in three wild cats for company. The uncle was still childless many years later.

A crow landed not ten feet away and began cawing loudly. He eyed it warily. He didn't want to be plucked at while he was still alive. It was loud and ugly. It hopped closer. Then the boy waved his stick at the crow. It cawed and withdrew to the large banyan tree.

Englishmen and nawabs, maybe that was the problem. When dharma collapses, famine is the result. What do they know about righteousness or virtue or religious duty? People must perform their caste duties—that is the basis of social and moral order. The thought of doing one's duties reminded him of his relatives again and filled him with rage. They call themselves Brahmins? Did they give no thought to their future births? Just this memory alone would make even a healthy man delirious!

He had been returning from the market—one of the stall keepers there was a pious and devout man—with a small bag of rice when he came upon them in the rear of the temple, whispering conspiratorially. They hushed up the moment he appeared. He demanded to know what they were whispering about in his temple. None of them wanted to talk, the blackguards! He glared at them until one spoke. The Maharaja of Burdwan, in order to secure religious merit for himself, had been making large grants of land to Brahmins. Many had already migrated inland, leaving the sacred river bank, to accept. They thought it was time they did, too.

"Were you just going to slink off without telling me?" he had screamed. "Just leave me to my fate? Is Burdwan sacred like this place? When you accept land, some of the merit he gains will be your loss! You must promise me not to leave." Each one solemnly promised not to leave. One by one they touched their hands to his feet. The next morning, they were all gone.

Reverend Sir lay on his cot, lost in delirium. Everything was collapsing. There was no one to leave his temple to. What would become of it? He began to look at his temple with a magnifying glass, examining every infinitesimal crack and pit in its surface. He walked around every side of it, then went inside and looked at every detail in every room. His vision had never been so acute. He realized this was a crystallized projection from his mind. Every atom in his body began to vibrate in sympathy with every atom in the temple. Reverend Sir lifted up and looked back down at the roof, rising higher and higher. He felt better now. He felt he had done his duty (as best he understood it) as well as he could. He felt happy and strong. Reverend Sir had never suspected, until now, that he could fly like this. He stretched out his arms for the sun.

Reverend Sir was slumped over, still in Padmasana, his forehead resting on the floor. His breathing was irregular. He was having a much harder time coming back to the present. That wandering yogi had given very detailed instruction on how to experience a past life, but apparently coming back to the present life was supposed to be much more automatic. He brought his arms forward and made a pillow out of his hands. He stayed there for a few moments, reflecting on what he had just gone through.

Returning to an earlier life as the priest of this temple no longer surprised him. But he still didn't know the reason for such a long standing and fierce attachment. Reverend Sir hoped his next trip back would be his last. He didn't know exactly how old this temple was, but he knew this wasn't an ancient temple.

He was very surprised, though, at how orthodox he was in this last experience, during what must have been the Great Bengal Famine of 1770. He remembered studying it in school. One third of the population of Bengal had died. It was really a little nothing, a little blip, compared to recent history. It was a long time ago. Probably everyone was more orthodox then.

He sat up straight and stretched his legs out, then bounced them up and down to get the circulation back. His clock said it was the same day, but much later in the afternoon. The rain had stopped and the sky looked mostly clear through the doorway. He slowly raised himself to his feet and walked out onto the platform. That fool cinema star existed only in patches and splotches now. A sudden curiosity overcame him. He recalled that he had floated up at the end of this trip back. Was this what happens when one dies? Reverend Sir looked up at the sky, shielding his eyes with his right palm. Was he the only one doing this? He looked and looked in every direction, but didn't see any floating people. Just a few crows (the sight of which made him shudder) and the dingy buildings of his neighborhood, their ground floors flooded. No nonfloating people, either.

Reverend Sir stayed out on the platform past nightfall, enjoying the open air, glad for a break in the rain, happy to just be able to walk around. He played memory games with himself, imagining all four of himselves sitting around a table, talking with each other.

Finally, he went to bed and slept quite well, little bothered by the other three people still carrying on outside.

The next morning, he felt an urge to put his affairs in order. He made his bed very carefully, then took stock of his food. It was getting low, and he had no desire to die of starvation again. He decided to put all his photographs and other personal effects into his small trunk. Reverend Sir held N. K.'s wedding photo in his hand, but felt nothing. What happened after that riot was horrible and depressing to contemplate.

The city was in shock after the riot. There was a tremendous shortage of wood to cremate the dead. The Hooghly was literally choked with half burned and totally unburned bodies. There were not many complaints from the shipping industry now, for few ships were braving the journey to this city of madness. The public health effort finally cracked at this point, and never recovered. Disease spread. Everyone now realized that there was no future for the city and stopped pretending that there was. People began to flow out—the poor by foot, the middle class by train and bus, the wealthy by plane and even chartered helicopters that landed quickly at designated spots, then took off before they could be mobbed. The last handful of British and the many Marwaris left in this manner. And it was not just the citizens of Calcutta. All of Bengal was on the move. Though some headed for Myanmar, most started walking to neighboring states in India.

But there was no room for them in the rest of India. The Indian Army had fortified the border.

Rumors of the fortification had been spreading through the city for some time. But rumors had become the daily diet of Calcutta, and no one could sort through them all. When columns of refugees started returning from the border, people began to believe them. Reverend Sir remembered how horrified and incredulous N. K. was at the news. He met with the other local officers of the Eastern

India Civil Engineering Authority. They decided to lead a march to the border. N. K. was in the front rank with his wife, who was holding their small daughter in her arms. He carried a large photograph of himself taken in Delhi when the Prime Minister and the entire Cabinet had given him India's highest honor for his service to the nation.

They never made it to the border. They unknowingly entered an automated field of fire, and were slaughtered. Millions died trying to find a hole in the border defenses. There were none.

The official announcement came in the form of millions of leaflets dropped by the Indian Air Force. Effectively immediately, West Bengal was no longer part of the Republic of India. No migration would be permitted. And that was the last image Bengalis had of the Government of India, once headquartered in Calcutta itself: a plane dropping leaflets, then disappearing over the horizon.

Then a very strange thing happened. Whereas the day before, everyone was sure that Calcutta and Bengal had no future, now everyone saw a brilliant future. A massive rally, peaceful this time, was held on the Maidan. Calcutta, it was declared, had once been the second city of the British Empire. Now it would be the first city of the world. At long last, imperialism had been thrown off! Without that burden on its shoulders, Bengal would rise up and join the first rank of nations. Whereas before, everyone had been content to let Bangladesh sink or swim on its own, now a huge sentiment developed to reunite all Bengalis, to end once and for all the outside world's strategy of divide and conquer, to finally throw off their colonial status. Bengal triumphant!

Those that had already left had seen it coming. The Mississippi Delta, the lower Nile, the great floodplains of Asia, were all inundated to various extents. But population in the U. S. was low, capital was available, food was available, and land was available. That was not the situation in the Ganga basin. The flooding was creating untold scores of millions of landless and homeless. Agriculture was disrupted throughout the world, due to the heat and drought caused by the warming. The food production from the inundated crop land was also lost. This had resulted in razor thin food reserves. And with world population at 12 billion, there was simply no place anywhere that would take them. More people, less food, no land. Bengal was not the only region to be abandoned. New Orleans and Rotterdam, seeing their interests diverge from the others, withdrew from Delta-Net. The moving speeches in the world's forums were replaced by much less generous ones.

Rioting became sporadic and desultory: The outside world was to blame, and they were not at hand. Many now retreated into cultural pursuits. The first big growth industry was the coffee houses. They were jammed with some of the world's most erudite and scholastic people, now no longer inconvenienced even in the slightest by having to deal with reality. Vast flood-control works were dreamed up and vetted by the dozen intellectuals at the table. World revolution was planned down to the smallest detail. The plans were so plausible, that one could believe all the planners had to do was step out on the sidewalk, and they would be at the very epicenter of the struggle. All sorts of intricate machinery (most depending on perpetual motion) to reverse the warming was invented and described with great precision. A few of the houses became so popular that they added more stories—which came in quite handy on days when the flooding was unusually bad.

The booksellers on College Street began to do banner business. Everyone had at least one more book that they just had to read before the end came. Since the Indian rupee was worthless—and there was no proper paper for a new Bengali currency—much of the exchange was by barter, with small crowds all giving their opinions on which books were really the most important to have read before one died. The publishers were hit hard by the shortage of paper.

Nevertheless, some volumes of poetry were published and snapped up by the public.

And what poetry! Reverend Sir almost swooned thinking of those leonine wonders. Although he was a religious man and tried to keep his mind in equilibrium, even his knees had buckled. Clarity, power, beauty, subtlety—all those and more. One could even think that the tragedy could be reversed by sheer force of will, incarnated in the versified word.

Next came the cinema. Always a haven from the harsh world outside, it now became more real than life itself. The movie palaces were always bursting, and god save the projectionist if the film should stop for any reason. If the theater flooded, people would calmly sit on the backs of the chairs. The wildest of fantasies were produced during this period; films no one would believe, yet everyone believed. His billboard had come from one of the very last of these films. He wondered whatever became of the star. Did he helicopter out, too?

Another blow to morale came when the zoo was overrun and all the animals were eaten. Even the zoo's most famous animals, the tigon (cross between a tiger and lion) and the litigon (cross between a lion and a tigon) were eaten. The sacking of the zoo created a small boomlet of nostalgia for the good old days. The Park Street cemetery became a favorite pilgrimage site for those mourning Calcutta's glory days as capital of the Raj. Lamentably, the liquefying ground was tilting the monuments askew, and even bringing a few caskets to the surface. There were always two crowds at the Victoria Memorial—one cheering the demise of this symbol of imperialism, the other dabbing at their eyes as this symbol of the glory days slowly sank into the mud. Bottles containing little messages asking the British to come back could be seen floating down the Hooghly now and then.

Perhaps the biggest industry of all (but a distant second to prostitution, of course, for what living being was not doing anything by now to survive?) was that of the gurus. Holy men were appearing from nowhere, and in great numbers. Most were giving peace of mind in exchange for a bit of food. Offerings, sacrifices and donations were made in stupefying amounts throughout the city. Why not? What else was left? A very large number of people came to the opinion that only Ganesha, the remover of obstacles, should be worshiped until this huge obstacle was removed. Ganesha was everywhere, even sold by the sidewalk vendors right next to little pieces of bleached coral from the dying reefs in the Bay of Bengal. Others were of the opinion that now was exactly not the time to abandon Calcutta's traditional deities, Kali and Durga, and that only by worshiping them would they come down to save the city. These two groups seldom came to blows, possibly because each thought that worship done in the other camp was a good insurance policy in case they themselves were wrong. Netaji was also propitiated constantly, the large sedan chair surrounded by lights so that he could find his way to it even in the dark. For, as everyone knew, he was a very old man by now, and would probably have some difficulty seeing with his physical eyes (though his leadership vision was surely as strong as ever).

One final thing often on people's lips was moksha—liberation—release from samsara. Though the best path to its achievement—jnana, bhakti, yoga, and so on—was endlessly debated, it was something more and more people wanted. More than an end to the warming, more than a huge dike to hold back the waters, more than to migrate to safety, more than the greatest poem in the world, more even than rebirth in heaven; many yearned for the wheel of birth and death to be broken, to never come back to this world of suffering. Everywhere one looked, people sought moksha and nothing else. Something was being stirred up. Past lives were coming to the surface. This cycle of existence was being brought to a close. Was this to be Bengal's revenge, he wondered?

Reverend Sir placed N. K.'s photo in the trunk and finished cleaning up. He would make what he hoped would be his final attempt today. He also wanted moksha. Reverend Sir would have to cut loose from this temple. He would go back four centuries.

He sat in the middle of the hut and began the procedure. He had to labor at it, but it came. Lighter and lighter, he rose into the air. He saw his temple below him, the Adiganga, the Kidderpore Docks to his left. As he rose, Calcutta became a vast jeweled bracelet with a black velvet river running down the middle. A billion billion diamonds sparkled in the sun, surrounded by an uncountable profusion of rubies and sapphires. The dazzling light pounded into his eyes and blasted to the back of his skull. As he started to descend, the jewels all changed to gold. He realized it was the golden color of ripening rice paddies. He landed with a thump, right in front of a splendid new temple.

Reverend Sir stood straight and tall, in the prime of his life. His clothes today were cut from the finest of muslin. He remembered a story—the man who told him swore it was true, but Reverend Sir thought it apocryphal—about the great Mughal emperor Aurangzeb, reproving one of his daughters for appearing in court naked, when she was in fact wearing seven layers of Bengali muslin. His muslin today was every bit as fine as that.

He stood on the front porch of his temple to be. It was being consecrated today after years of meticulous construction. His force of will had shepherded it through innumerable snags and setbacks. It was intended to rival nearby Kalighat, and he thought it would. The astrologers had conferred for months to determine the most auspicious moment to have the consecration ceremony—in view of the changed circumstances—and today was it. Hundreds came to be a part of it.

Sitting before him in long rows on the grass were Brahmins from the neighboring villages: Govindapur, Sutanuti, Kalikata and others. They were honoring the occasion by feasting to capacity. Behind them, and separated by a considerable distance to avoid polluting the Brahmins, were important local people. To the right of those sat a group of pilgrims. To the left sat a few officials from Aurangzeb's court. Farthest of all in the back sat two groups of merchants; Malays and Chinese from upcountry on the left; Dutch, Danish, French, Armenians, Portuguese and British on the right. Enfolding this large cosmopolitan assemblage was the exuberant foliage of lower Bengal. Tucked away in the greenery were thatched cottages peeking out here and there. Beyond the cottages were the swaying golden fields of ripening paddy. It was a tropical idyll, sensuous and ripe.

The only problem marring this idyll was the drying river bed nearby. The braided Ganga had flowed by, strong and sacred, when construction had begun. Then just last year, the river shifted its course. The waters shrank to a comparative trickle, and no one knew if or when they would return. Much discussion took place about what to do. Perhaps a little coaxing was all that was needed, thought Reverend Sir at the time. He decided to go ahead and finish the temple.

The priest in charge of the consecration came up to him. "Now is the time," he said, and led Reverend Sir into the sanctum sanctorum.

The consecration began. Many mantras were spoken; all with precise intonation, exacting gestures and perfect timing. Much melted ghee was used. Oil lamps and burning incense were everywhere. Then, at exactly the right moment, one additional sentence was added to the ceremony, a sentence that was not usually there.

"I vow to stay at this temple until the Ganga returns," said Reverend Sir. Something twitched inside him when he said it.

The ceremony resumed. It went perfectly. When it was over, an ordinary building had become a temple, and a statue of a goddess, a goddess.

Reverend Sir walked outside onto the porch. He felt elated. He had done it. He closed his eyes and felt light and airy. He saw with a shock when he opened his eyes that he was floating upwards. Then he realized what was happening.

"No! No!" he screamed. "I want to stay here! Let me go back!" Reverend Sir thrashed and clawed in midair, but it had no effect, and nobody heard him. He rose higher and higher and his perfect world shrunk away beneath him. He started to sob.

Reverend Sir lay flat on his stomach, saliva dripping out of the corner of his mouth. He was utterly exhausted from the stress of being ripped away from his past life. He couldn't go back again, even if he wanted to. He couldn't even open his eyes. Reverend Sir drifted off to sleep.

The next morning, he awoke still lying face down on the floor. His saliva had dried and flies were skittering around on it. Reverend Sir wiped the side of his mouth and sat up.

He remembered that golden moment when this temple was new. He was stupefied that a vow could have such a powerful and lasting effect. The ancient texts were full of heroes and heroines, gods and goddesses all making powerful vows. He had always assumed it was literary license. Now he found himself a prisoner of his own vow! He rubbed his temples, then stood up.

Reverend Sir grabbed a rag and wiped up the dried saliva. His rations would run out today. He looked around his hut. Everything was still in its place. He picked up one of his Sanskrit books and walked out onto the platform.

The cinema star was gone and the platform was waterlogged and warping. He walked over to one edge. The water had risen over six feet since Mr. Bose and Mr. Sen had tied up their boat. A few more days of rain, and it would flood the platform and his hut. He reached down and tore off a piece of soggy wood and threw it as far as he could.

"I don't believe in vows anymore, do you hear?" he yelled. No one was there to hear. Reverend Sir sat down and looked into the murky water, trying to find his reflection.

Perhaps the Ganga has returned, he thought to himself. True, it was not as he imagined it four centuries ago. But there was water everywhere, including the old dry riverbed. He pondered the situation for a long while. How does one know such things for sure? He finally concluded that he was now released from his vow; that he had stuck with this temple through many lives until the Ganga had returned.

He was free now. He wanted to be free forever. But he still wasn't sure how to do it. Although the visions of a sparkling Calcutta were very seductive, he was afraid that if he used the technique the yogi taught him, he would end up in some past or future life, condemned to turn forever in the wheel of birth and death.

Reverend Sir opened up his Sanskrit book, the Skanda Purana, to a verse about the banks of the Ganga he had often turned to in the past. It read:

"Any person who dies here goes to heaven; he has no rebirth."

What puzzled him about this verse was the word heaven. By heaven, did it mean an incredibly blissful abode that lasted for countless ages, but that eventually came to an end, and therefore led to a subsequent rebirth on this earthly plane? That is what he thought the word heaven meant. But then the second part categorically states that there is no rebirth, in which case heaven is more like moksha, the release from birth and rebirth. Moksha is what Reverend Sir wanted now.

He wanted to die here and now, to be released. He didn't want to starve again. Perhaps drowning would be the way to go. But currents in the water might carry him away from the old river bed. Should he lash himself down? But suicide was a sin. Surely that might nullify everything!

He heard a splashing sound and looked up. The crocodile had returned. It had a compassionate look in its eyes. Reverend Sir did not shake his head this time. The crocodile swam closer.

Older Patterns

This story was sparked by an article in the February 1994 Atlantic *entitled "The Coming Anarchy." It was a horrifying picture of global social disintegration and regression.*

Several people have remarked that this story has a journalistic tone to it and that it's unclear what position the author takes. My position is that the story is like a Rorschach test. If you think the situation in the story is undesirable, then you passed. If you think it is desirable, then perhaps the transition described is already in progress . . .

George wasn't sure, exactly—and friends sometimes asked, friends being the way they are—why he liked black women best. He just did. Some like Latinas. Some like Asians. Some like all kinds. Some like only their own kind. He liked blacks. And today was the day.

He picked up his desk phone and punched the button for the doorman. It rang only once.

"Yes, Mr. Smith?" asked Abi.

"Abi, my dear friend Mademoiselle de Bougainville will be arriving this afternoon; the one I spoke to you about earlier? Yes, that one. Please show her to my elevator without delay. And don't forget: no entries in the security logs," he told Abi.

"Yes Mr. Smith."

George had been giving Abi larger and larger tips every Christmas for the last five years, in anticipation of this day. Abi now owed him more than he owed the building's management. He would handle it.

George put the phone down and looked back at his computer's screen. He spent 90 minutes every afternoon tending to his portfolio. They were the best 90 minutes of his day: cool, automated efficiency; total command and control. A few years back he had made an obscene amount with synthetics. Nowadays, he was back to basic value investing. It was a good thing he had a way with money, because the final payment due on delivery was quite substantial.

He finalized his list of buy and sell orders, executed, then waited a few moments for the confirmations to come back. Good. He had caught the uptick he needed for his short. Next, he went to City Events to look over the coming theater season. Hmm…the usual mix of old warhorses and new hopefuls. Season tickets or not? The theater district was such a war zone these days. That reminded him to check Shopping for his new walking stick (with taser). Good news here, too. Due for delivery in three days. It was just what he needed to keep the rabble off him. Finally, he put the computer to sleep. His legs were rubbery when he stood up. God this was going to be great!

He closed the door to his office (the only modern room in his apartment) and walked down the central hallway and into the living room. He was so nervous! Had he forgotten anything? All 21 rooms were freshly cleaned. The kitchen was stocked. Everybody thought he was out of town. Even emergency calls would get his voice mail. The three rooms of his private suite were in excellent repair—no one should have to visit them for years to come. One (or two) could retreat there when the cleaning service came.

He sat down on the harpsichord bench. Autumn sunlight streamed through the windows. The entire apartment was decorated in Louis XVI. *Real* Louis XVI. Most of his friends had larger places, but none were decorated in the superb taste that his was. His father had assembled most of the collection; George had completed it.

His father. This day would never have arrived if that old fart hadn't finally died. George had loved him dearly, and even admired his ethics to a point. But his father never realized—never felt in his gut—that all that United States of America everybody-is-a-person crap was passé. This was a new century and a new world. Now George was getting to live the way he wanted to live; the way everyone else was starting to live; the way people used to live; the way Homo sapiens were meant to live.

George wasn't making this up just because it was convenient. He had done the research. For millennia, males possessed as many females as they could afford. The great imperial harems of China, Rome, India, and so on, had held thousands of women. Men of lesser status and wealth had possessed fewer. (Of course, this was long before alimony and palimony, George noted bitterly.) It was only with the coming of industrialization and democracy that the aristocratic estates began to shrink and disappear. This great arc of history reached its peak in the United States during World War II and the Fifties. As the postindustrial economy emerged, however, society began to demassify and restratify; to go back to older patterns.

In fact, George reflected further, he was really doing her a tremendous favor—saving her from disease and poverty and who knows what else. And it wasn't like he was building up an entire harem (which surely a man of his position deserved). He just wanted one. Albeit a perfect one.

He first started sensing this revival in party talk some years ago. He could tell by the way people were talking that some of them were speaking from their own experience—even though they were phrasing it as though they had seen it on tabloid TV. So he very discreetly made inquiries in the most hypothetical of terms. Then he made even more discreet inquiries in less hypothetical terms.

He was stunned by how much the best cost. Even now he shook his head from time to time. At first he tried to do it on the cheap, with that bitch from D. C.

George stood up and started pacing to calm himself. God, did that blow up in his face! What kind of shit do they teach in the school system there, anyway? The bitch went wild when she figured out the situation. Busted up a whole roomful of antiques. He had to call security to get rid of her, then pay them to keep it quiet. It was a close call. That's why you never see Americans employed on cruise ships—they just don't understand service.

So he went back to his connection. George arranged a long lunch together at a restaurant in the Village. It had private booths, and George seldom came to the Village. He didn't think he would be recognized. His connection was elegantly dressed and treated George to the restaurant's finest. They talked businessman to businessman, going through the costs one by one. Gradually, George realized that it was expensive to buy because it was expensive to provide. His connection laid it all out for him.

"The good news is that the cost of the girls is zero: they are as common as ants, and they're simply snatched," said his connection matter-of-factly. "The bad news is that our business is conducted in a difficult environment and the development process is very lengthy. Transportation also has to be arranged."

George nibbled on his porcini mushrooms. Excellent sauce. His connection continued.

"First, we have a vast network of operatives from Dakar to Lagos looking for talent. Those guys all need to be fed, clothed, armed, equipped and inoculated. It's just one big, sprawling superslum, really. There are constant turf battles between private armies, the drug cartels, mercenaries, village chiefs and so on. There is no law. There is no order."

"What about the governments?" George asked. (He had assumed that it was more a question of just paying off the right officials.) His connection smiled wanly and topped off George's goblet.

"It's really us and the drug cartels that run things, surrounded by all the small fry," his connection said. "The governments have only nominal control over the coastal trading posts—Conakry, Abidjan, etcetera—during the day. They're actually just shantytown states, but they do serve a useful purpose."

"What purpose?" asked George. He realized he was getting off track, but he found this fascinating. It seemed that just as the West was returning to older patterns, so was Africa. His connection was describing a return to the brutality and chaos of colonial—even precolonial—days. He also wondered if maybe he shouldn't take a flier with the "have fun" part of his portfolio. True, the risks were high, but the potential rewards . . .

The waiter showed up with the main course. His connection had ordered filet mignon, which looked delicious. George had ordered a lobster bouillabaisse. It looked equally delicious. His connection continued, happy to oblige his curiosity.

"As fronts, of course," he replied. "Think of the trade flows. People and drugs flow out of Africa, money and food flow in. Very few people in America realize that the wealthiest men in the world live in Africa."

"What?" sputtered George, confused. "Why, why don't they do something about the conditions there?"

"Why would they want to change things? They are doing quite nicely with things the way they are." His connection sat there a moment, still and unblinking, to see if George could muster a response. Then he went on. "Anyway, with wealth comes power. That power can be projected abroad. Africa's vast food requirements naturally have to be met with imports, since organized agriculture is impossible. Most of those imports are free, buried in foreign aid budgets under 'technical assistance.'"

His connection seemed to derive tremendous amusement from the phrase "technical assistance." It was obvious that George was even more confused now, so his connection explained.

"You see? All those young men with machine guns mounted on their vehicles? They are called technicals, so, when we give them money, it is called..." and his body shook for a few moments while he enjoyed the pun again.

"It works out well. The American farmers get paid by the taxpayers, and we see that the farm-state senators also do quite well. Naturally, it helps to have a 'government' to receive this assistance."

George was starting to feel a bit uneasy, boyhood lessons about patriotism from his father coming back to him, perhaps. His connection enjoyed seeing him squirm, but didn't let it show.

"We're even able to block satellite surveillance, some of the time. And there is one area of high tech where Africans are the absolute leaders. Can you guess it?"

George shook his head.

"Cryptography. Naturally, a wired system cannot be maintained in a state of anarchy, so all communications are wireless. Since Africa's two biggest exports are illegal, communications have to be encrypted."

The conversation paused for a moment when the waiter brought two crème bruléts and two coffees. His connection suddenly became somber as he looked at his cup.

"In my father's time, coffee was a big foreign exchange earner for us." He stirred in a bit of cream, then carefully placed his spoon on the saucer and grasped his cup. The color of his coffee now matched his hand. "Not anymore."

"In any case," he said, anxious to wrap up, "if our operatives spot some nice little pieces around eight or nine years of age, they're snatched and taken to a facility in the interior—more overhead. Then they have to be cured of a myriad of diseases (some are incurable, regrettably, and are culled almost immediately), fed, clothed and trained. Basic training consists of the fundamentals of civilization—eradicating habits of communalism, animism, and so on. Mostly they just have to grow up. The ones that don't pan out are marketed within Africa to defray expenses."

"The ones that grow into export quality need more food, more intensive training and memory implants. If one orders far enough in advance…"

He pulled a small booklet out of his vest pocket and flipped to George's page. "…as you have, then one can even specify the memories and some of the personality. More time and expense."

"Finally, they have to be readied for travel and then sent via a rather circuitous route, since direct routes to the States no longer exist. Most go through Europe. So they need phony papers and tickets. Bribes and more operatives to pay. Then delivery to your very door. And since this is all still illegal—for some quaint reason, no doubt," he said, smiling, "a risk premium is tacked on every step of the way."

And so George learned why it was expensive. It was up to the potential customer to decide if it was worth it. George decided that it was.

The buzzer sounded.

"Mr. Smith, Mademoiselle de Bougainville has arrived and will be at your door shortly," announced Abi. He clicked off before George could answer.

Jesus, this is it! George went to his front door and looked through the peep hole into his elevator's private foyer. The elevator door opened. She stepped out and rang the bell. He looked at her for a moment. He was speechless. George opened the door.

"Bonjour, Mr. Smith!"

"Bonjour, Mademoiselle de Bougainville!"

"My, what a handsome man you are!"

"How sweet of you to say so! Please, come in," said George. He showed her into the sitting room, after taking her cape and hanging it up.

"Oh, what very fine taste you have, Mr. Smith!"

She was dressed in the highest of haute couture. Her Parisian accent was perfect. The flight was quite acceptable, yes. This crisp fall weather suited her quite well, thank you. She was very happy to find some time for the Upper East Side on this hectic business trip. She was delighted that their mutual acquaintance had suggested she come visit him. Yes, she would love a tour of the apartment.

And so it went like that for the rest of the afternoon and early evening. George had never seen such a perfect creature in his entire life. Nor had he ever had such delightfully refined conversation. Everything about her was exquisite. Her eyes were almond shaped, her nose as elegant as Cleopatra's, her lips as full and succulent as any movie star's. This was just incredible. He even pinched himself once, to see if it hurt. It did. This was real.

As the evening wore on, George noticed that she was starting to repeat herself. This implant had reached its limit. He concluded it must be time to trigger the main implant. He surreptitiously pulled the slip of paper out of his shirt pocket. His connection had said it was very important to get it right the first time. George raised his hand to interrupt.

"Yes, but I am the master and you are my slave," he read aloud.

Her eyes went glassy and she slumped for a moment. Then she stood up quietly, and methodically removed her clothing, piece by piece. When she finished, she had nothing on but a loincloth and four gold bangles—two around her wrists, two around her ankles. The loincloth was a few inches square in the front, nothing at all in the back.

He looked at her with rapt attention as she stood there. Not an ounce of fat anywhere. Her biceps were finely sculpted, her breasts so firm. Her thighs were for bounding through the savanna; her ass, perfect.

She began to walk slowly around the living room, as if she had never laid eyes on it before—as if she had never seen anything like it before. Her body was so lithe, her motions so fluid and effortless. She was the noble savage George had thirsted for all his life.

He knew now that she was his forever, and would never leave this apartment again. Everything between them would always be the way he wanted it to be. He led her to the divan, laid her face down, and started licking her black ass.

He was in heaven.

Online

This is the first story I wrote, in August of 1994, with a female protagonist. I had a lot of fun writing the dialogue. I tried to capture the excitement and chaos and unknown possibilities of cyberspace in the mid-Nineties as the larger public rushed in for the first time.

Sally plumped herself down in the chair opposite me. She fussed with my camera a bit, then blew her nose. Been crying, definitely. Not sleeping well either. She looked like hell.

Sally put her tissue away and looked straight at me. "I can trust you, can't I? I mean, it's your job to listen to people and help them out, right?"

"Absolutely," I said.

"Because I've heard about people coming out of therapy more messed up than when they went into it. I don't want that to happen to me—and I don't want this to drag on forever, either," she said, looking at me warily. "I just need a little help to get over this . . . this . . . " Upon which she started to sob again.

"I understand," I said. "I have only your well-being at heart. My success rate is very high. As for how long it will take, well, that depends on so many variables. What exactly is troubling you?"

"And this is all confidential, too? I mean, you don't talk to other specialists and laugh about it over lunch and everything, right?" asked Sally, wanting to believe in me. The lady was really taking this hard. I adopted the dulcet tones of a FM broadcaster.

"Sally, I am completely and totally qualified to handle all but the criminally insane. And we're not that, are we?" Sally smiled and giggled a bit through her tears. "Everything you and I say will be held in strict confidence. No one will ever know what we talked about—or even that we talked at all." Sally looked relieved.

"Now then," I continued, "the more you open up, the quicker we can get to the bottom of things and put your life back on track. Would you like to start today? Or wait for another time?"

Sally blew her nose one last time and looked braver. She was really quite an attractive brunette. I felt something like pity for her. She straightened herself up and started in.

"Honest to God, I had no idea—and I mean, no idea—it would turn out the way it did. The whole thing started completely by accident—I wasn't even looking for it! It was around the beginning of the year. Jack was already starting to work late—he's an accountant— tax season coming up, you know—and I was on our online service, checking out the news, our portfolio, and so on. The usual stuff I did online. Then I realized I still had a lot of time left in my account for the month. So I decided to check out some other areas of the service to see what they were like. Just curious. And I just loved our service—so fun and safe and everything. Thought I might find something worthwhile. So I went over to the Silicon Spa. That's how it all began . . ."

Sally clicked on the Spa icon and found herself in its atrium. A long list of suites appeared. She read down the list:

Bi Married M4M
What RU Wearing
F Needs M in Uniform
Epilepsy Support
HairyM4HairyM
Truth or Dare
Abuse Survivors

Young and Depressed
Married and Curious
Vampires Welcome
I Hate Everything
MBM4MWF4 Affair
Number 221B Baker St
Love Long Hair
M4F4 Dark Fantasies
Stupid People No SPAM
Wicked Witches
Out of Bath Dress Me
Get Me Ready for Hubby
Doctors Office
Id Love to Show You
Sincere Honest People
Cops Who Flirt
Philosophy Chat
M4F in2 Piercing

Hmm. Who would've ever thought there could be so many combinations of people and preferences. Sally wondered if she should take a look in any of them. Why not? It doesn't get any safer than this, she thought. Why not try Married and Curious? That's what she was. She clicked and a very confused group conversation appeared on her screen, line by line:

Whoooahh: PS I'm a girl today
SouthernGent: You change gender regularly?
Bill2235: bye–bye
Whoooahh: NO, just share this thing with someone else!
SouthernGent: Oh. I thought that your problem might be connected with your sex. Sorry.
Whoooahh: I have no problems with sex.
Whoooahh: Sorry if I offended anyone
Sirreal108: I feel compelled to point out that this failure is entirely due to human error.
HappyLetcher: Hi everyone
SexySue2U: What's the matter hon your man don't give you that?
Quarterback: gee, this suite is exciting
Jim6Gun: Hi everyone
Syzygy223: What's the point? Isn't the marriage enough?

IntenseGuy: Sorry. Been married so long, I forgot how to flirt!

Jim6Gun: hello...

HappyLetcher: hi

FunAsUCanB: I can get it anywhere I want!! :>

Jim6Gun: flirt flirt flirt :)

SexySue2U: If not, you're talking to the right guy

Quarterback: first you say something nice

IntenseGuy: I think you've got a great typing voice.

Jim6Gun: I hate typing

IntenseGuy: You know what they say if they can't take a joke...

SomeFun69: would anyone like to go for a ride?

Califelvis: anybody here seen UPleesMeNow

UPleesMeNow: {{{{{{{{{{   Califelvis   }}}}}}}}}}}

SomeFun69: she's in the back of the ford

Califelvis: OH   UPleesMeNow
{{{{{{{{{{{{{{{{{{{{{{{{{{{UPleesMeNow}}}}}}}}}}}}}}}}}}}}}}}}}}}

UPleesMeNow: it's not true

SexySue2U: Let's do the Age/Sex thing.

XpertLvr4U: time for a sex/age/state/sexual preference check

XpertLvr4U: I want a woman in heat

XpertLvr4U: for a one night stand

XpertLvr4U: any volunteers?

Califelvis: UPleesMeNow i miss you {{{{{{{{{{{{{UPleesMeNow}}}}}}}}}}}}}
send you a rose--
                          --<-<---<@

SomeFun69: are you guys in love?

CubFan8312: We are all in love.

UPleesMeNow: with ourselves

UPleesMeNow: lol

SomeFun69: boring!!!!!!!!!!!!!!!

Larry315: Does it get anymore exciting than this ??

ImaTenStud: __/ __/__/ drinks on me ....let's party

Lothario27: so .... are there any other married females flirting here
tonight?

CubFan8312: lol

2Right: no

2Right: yes

CubFan8312: NO or YES?

HunEBuns: Married?

2Right: yes

MMMBaby: That's a requirement to be here, isn't it?

HunEBuns: oh yeah I lost my mind for a moment.

It seemed like an utterly hopeless way of communicating to her.
She clicked on the list of people in the suite:

XpertLvr4U
HunEBuns
ImaTenStud
SweetLady31
IntenseGuy
FunAsUCanB
WondrPuppy
Jim6Gun
UPleesMeNow
Lothario27
MMMBaby
Syzygy223
Sirreal108
KCQT
HappyLetcher
MayIPlease
SexySue2U
2Right
SomeFun69
Whoooahh
Califelvis
Larry315
CubFan8312
SouthernGent
Quarterback

Where on earth do people get their handles, she wondered. Sally
clicked on the information button for ImaTenStud:

Name:	ImaTenStud
Residence:	Anywhere you want me to be!
Date of Birth:	Virgo… (NOT!)
Gender:	All Male
Marital Status:	Swinging Single
Job:	Warehouse Supervisor
Hobbies:	Motorcycling, Football, SEX!!
Motto:	I want someone that does it all!!

No wonder that guy is single—no subtlety. She clicked another one:

Name:	Larry315
Residence:	Des Moines, IA
Date of Birth:	Sept. 1954
Gender:	Male
Marital Status:	Married
Job:	Most of the time
Hobbies:	Not much
Motto:	Live life to the fullest. Don't take anything for granted.

Another loser. Then Sally suddenly realized that her own bio was available to everybody else and was a little too revealing for the kind of thing she was doing. What if one of the other account executives at work found her in the Silicon Spa? She hastily called up her bio and modified it to read as follows:

Name:	SoftNSweet
Residence:	Houston, TX
Date of Birth:	1964 (a fine year)
Gender:	Female
Marital Status:	Married
Job:	Account Executive
Hobbies:	Sunbathing, swimming, bodybuilding and SEXercise!
Motto:	Want to get naughty with me?

There. She liked her new identity. And it was all true—just exaggerated and not too specific.

Sally looked back at the group conversation.

MMMBaby: Mavis Beacon isn't welcome here.
ImaTenStud: {{{{{Hugs for everyone}}}}}}}}}}}
WondrPuppy: the 'revolving door' effect
HunEBuns: everyone does the quick cruise and on to another suite
CubFan8312: 3...2...1...And Welcome to Morgue Night
CubFan8312: Tonight's program includes an impromptu net-a-thon for autism!
CubFan8312: I hate when I found out I've been chatting in my sleep
SweetLady31: ***** to all the handsome married men in the suite!

HappyLetcher: Any other women besides Sweet?
KCQT: <----me woman
IntenseGuy: my damn keyboard keeps locking up on me....
WondrPuppy: may I take a dip??
SouthernGent: ok
Jim6Gun: jump right in!
WondrPuppy: >>splash<<
MayIPlease: So sorry, I'm off to Singapore to be voluntarily caned for my transgression.
Whoooahh: Sweet, want to go private?
SweetLady31: No, I want to share myself with all in this suite!
Quarterback: ::::walking over to Sweet.:::::
SweetLady31: ::::taking QB's hand:::::
Quarterback: ::::::picking her up in my arms::::::
Quarterback: ::::sweeping her off her feet!::::::
Quarterback: ::::::running out of the suite::::::
IntenseGuy: this suite has one foot over the cliff and the other grabbin' air ...
SexySue2U: I don't love em and leave em...I flirt
XpertLvr4U: was that so hard?
Syzygy223: GREetiNGs FrOM CalIforNIa!! Easter Eggs for everybody!...
(~) (=) (#) ($) (+)
FunAsUCanB: but this brings out sheer honesty
2Right: You right Fun... Refreshing too.
FunAsUCanB: without the facade of looks or appearances to get over
SomeFun69: You know how easy it is for a guy or girl to sign on as the opposite sex?
SomeFun69: they like to play jokes on people.
FunAsUCanB: yes, there are weirdoes here
IntenseGuy: Only thing I can say is you never know...you never know
2Right: Well that's why one is careful....
FunAsUCanB: yes, careful, but keep an open mind... this is supposed to be fun too!
FunAsUCanB: we only go through life once
2Right: Takes time and then one day ya know it's true.... Ya gain trust and then things fall into place
KCQT: Hi again everyone ;)
HappyLetcher: Runs after lady, jumping to make a flying tackle
Califelvis: smiles, hold up a card reading 9.5 (tough judge)
WondrPuppy: So who's alone in here?
ImaTenStud: MOI!!!
MayIPlease: Stud, I think we *all* are....
MMMBaby: I wish I could slap stupid people.
KCQT: your hand would be beet red right now
SweetLady31: what differentiates an idiot from a cretin or a moron?

MMMBaby: "I'd like a Big Mac and a Large Coke." "Did you want fries?"
"DID I ORDER ANY FRIES, DAMN IT?!!!!!"
Jim6Gun: I'm not only tired of idiots...I'm exhausted
Jim6Gun: met a few today....
SexySue2U: i meet a lot at work!
Lothario27: SoftNSweet--How soft?
2Right: If we're discussing about discussing then we are discussing something.
2Right: I'm a telecommunications Consultant.
2Right: Big title but not worth it.

Seeing her handle come up on her screen startled Sally. What should she do? She decided to send a private message back and start up a conversation.

SoftNSweet: Very soft
Lothario27: How sweet?
SoftNSweet: Very sweet
Lothario27: Are you really a woman?
SoftNSweet: Yes...last time I checked. <g> What about yourself?
Lothario27: No. Male, married, cute.
SoftNSweet: Cute, huh?
Lothario27: *Very* cute.
SoftNSweet: Me too.....cute, that is.
Lothario27: Married?
SoftNSweet: Married....no kids
Lothario27: How long have you been married?
SoftNSweet: 4 years in May.
Lothario27: What is your husband doing right now?
SoftNSweet: working late
Lothario27: What kind of bodybuilding do you do?
SoftNSweet: 2 hours minimum.....strength and endurance training......
punching bag.....sparring....weight lifting......
Lothario27: Wow. How tall and how much do you weigh?
SoftNSweet: 5'6.......135 lbs
Lothario27: Are you blonde?
Lothario27: And how about your eyes?
SoftNSweet: Light brown hair/Dark brown eyes
Lothario27: And I LOVE brown eyes.
SoftNSweet: what about you??
Lothario27: I'm 6'0 and 180. Very well-muscled, thick hair, olive colored skin (hey, I'm Italian!) Also, I lied earlier.......I'm extremely handsome, not cute.

SoftNSweet: that gives me a good idea......VERY nice.....
Lothario27: You must look GREAT when you're working out. Do you have nice leotards?
SoftNSweet: of course
Lothario27: Deep tan or fair skinned?
SoftNSweet: I have a GREAT tan
Lothario27: Mmm...I bet you do.
SoftNSweet: aw shucks....you are makin' me blush
Lothario27: You mean, I'm bringing a little heat to your cheeks? You look lovely that way.
SoftNSweet: why thank you, you smooth talker

It went on like that for hours, but it got less and less silly and much deeper instead. He felt like a kindred soul: very special, sensitive, articulate, caring. Finally, Sally logged off and got ready for bed. Jack was beat when he came home and had already turned in. Sally lay next to him for a long time thinking about her conversation with Lothario27. Even though it was just words on a screen, it seemed so immediate, so palpable. And he certainly seemed nice. And really handsome. And hot.

Sally felt a little guilty and sheepish the next morning. She decided during an unusually tedious staff meeting (the kind where people who don't know anything yammer at people who don't care about anything) that she wouldn't log on tonight. Her life was great. Why mess it up?

But when evening rolled around and Jack was working late again, she couldn't help going online. While she was checking her email, he found her—and she immediately lost it.

Lothario27: Hi, sweet stuff! Greetings from Boston.
SoftNSweet: Boston?? TOOOO cold.......love the Texas HEAT
Lothario27: You love to be hot?
SoftNSweet: Definitely
Lothario27: Sizzling, steaming, sweaty, dripping hot?
SoftNSweet: Definitely.........
Lothario27: Burning up, can't stand it any longer hot?
SoftNSweet: You got it Lothario27......

Lothario27: So hot and juicy a man could just come right up and slide right into you without a problem hot?
SoftNSweet: I think you've hit the nail on the "head" Lothario27
Lothario27: GOD DAMN you sound good!
SoftNSweet: and I feel even better
Lothario27: I'm speechless....If I smoked, I'd be lighting a cigarette just about now...
SoftNSweet: ha ha.......very cute
Lothario27: Do you have firm little buns?
SoftNSweet: VERY
Lothario27: Ooooh!!
Lothario27: Enough to squeeze and hang onto until it hurts?
SoftNSweet: until it hurts BADLY
Lothario27: Until little welts come up and I leave fingernail impressions in you?
SoftNSweet: You get into this pain thing don't ya?
Lothario27: Not really. I'm sure it's your influence!
SoftNSweet: I'm flattered
Lothario27: You should be. You're terrific!
Lothario27: So what's your husband doing right now?
SoftNSweet: working late....
Lothario27: I see... and you're here talking to me--you *naughty* little thing!
SoftNSweet: love to be "naughty" with or without him
Lothario27: "If you can't be with the one you love, honey,..."
SoftNSweet: I hear ya
Lothario27: Let me finish undoing your bra (I was in such a hurry earlier).
Lothario27: Mmm. Very Nice.
Lothario27: Ask me anything, sugar britches.
SoftNSweet: sugar britches?? Are you sure you aren't from Tx?
Lothario27: Heard it in a movie.
SoftNSweet: LOL........so where's the wife?
Lothario27: Out with her girlfriends.
SoftNSweet: Why not come to a beautiful brunette....
Lothario27: Mmm...brunettes. I'm looking you over front and back.
Lothario27: Maybe I'll roll you over on your stomach...
Lothario27: Take your left foot and pull it to the left...
Lothario27: Take your right foot and pull it to the right...

From there it just went straight downhill. Sally started logging on every single night to talk with him. She was glad the service was on her credit card, because Jack would sure the hell want to know what was going on if he saw the bill. They didn't even bother with the rest of the Spa or the open suites. They just went straight to a private suite and did it all.

Lothario27 was quite imaginative, and would often dream up exotic and erotic locations for the two of them. Her favorite was the night this message was delivered in her email to set up that night's activities in the suite:

From: Lothario27
To: SoftNSweet
Subj: Come away with me

I must have you again. I have told my wife I am going overseas on business—to London. I don't think she suspects yet. I have already booked full round trip tickets for both of us for next month. Yours will arrive shortly at work. Please have your colleagues cover for you while you're gone. I am going from London to Morocco three days ahead of you to make final arrangements. Your flight is from Houston to Paris. (I included a few—well, ten actually—thousand dollars with your ticket for you to do some shopping there. I hope that's all right with you.) I'll have someone meet your flight from Paris at the airport in Casablanca and drive you down the coast to Marrakech..................Your car wends its way down the coastal highway, the Atlas Mountains on your left, the azure blue Atlantic on your right. You brought some reading with you, but you can think only of me. As you approach Marrakech in the late afternoon, the driver turns off the highway and starts to zig zag up a mountain spur, dodging a few goats and camels. Finally he brings the car to a halt in front of a charming old French villa. You get out and he drives off. You stand there quivering with anticipation. You walk up the steps and through the door. It is pleasantly cool and dim inside. You see a lighted archway at the end of the hallway. You walk through it and step onto a rooftop garden..................You see me sitting in a rattan chair, an iced drink in my hand. You walk up behind me and gently put your hand on my shoulder. I put my hand up to hold yours. We remain that way for a moment, silent. Faint sounds can be heard from the town below: bargaining in the bazaar, a mother calling her children in for dinner, music from a wedding perhaps. Very subtle and provocative smells also waft upwards: jasmine, sandalwood (or something like sandalwood), freshly cut melons....................I stand up to hold you in my arms. We kiss. Then a spark flashes in your eye, and I know what you are thinking. We look around. No one can see us on our secluded rooftop. We take off each other's clothes and stand side by side, a caressing breeze now coming off the ocean and up the mountain side. I point to the moon coming over the mountains. It is a perfect moment. I lead you back through the archway and into the master chamber..............You see before you a large circular bed, smothered with luxurious pillows of many shapes and sizes. The late afternoon sun is diffused by layers of translucent fabrics hanging from the ceiling. You realize, now, that you are to be queen of my harem........... Next to the bed is a table. On the table is an ancient silver platter, fully four feet long, detailed with extraordinary filigree. On the platter sit delectable fruits, dates, figs, juices, wines, water and ice. You walk over to it and also see several bottles of body oil. You pick one up and take off the top to smell it. It is transcendental............ ......I am laying on the bed. My powerfully muscled body is laid out for tasting like the fruit on the platter. I am completely yours. Have your way with me.

That was a blistering one. The cutest part was that, afterwards, he even sent a sweet little ending:

From: Lothario27
To: SoftNSweet
Subj: Memories 4 U

The days of bliss now come to an end. Our last flight together takes us back to Boston. We keep the blanket spread across our laps. My right hand seldom rests on top of it. You have an enigmatic smile for the entire flight. The stewardess suspects, I think, because she gives you a knowing little smile every time she looks at you..............I walk you to your gate for the flight back to Houston. After our days at the villa, the hustle and bustle of Logan International is surreal. Our final kiss. I give you a bundle of photos of me, then say goodbye...............I watch from the observation lobby as your flight takes off for Texas. Then I get my baggage and hail a cab in the rain, alone.

Note: Go to the Spa's Photo Shoppe and look under my name. I have a bunch of photos there for you. ;–)

She downloaded the photos and brought them up on her screen. Gorgeous. Just gorgeous. A girl really couldn't ask for more.

That Saturday, Sally brought their new digital camera to the bedroom for a photo shoot. She had learned how to set these up at work.
Only today, it would be just her on both sides of the camera.

She screwed the camera to the tripod and played around with the
lighting levels for a while. It had to be soft and sexy, but not too dark.
Then she got out the satin sheets and pillows. It had been a long time
since she had used these with Jack, she realized. Sally slipped out
of her clothes and went to the closet to pick out her sexiest piece of
lingerie. Definitely the red one. She put it on and looked at herself
in the full-length mirror. She did look good.

Sally climbed onto the bed and struck some poses for the camera.
Then she got up and looked at the first batch. Too restrained, she
decided. She needed a gimmick to get into the flow of it. Then she
remembered that the voice activated shutter was also programma-
ble, so she changed the activation phrase to "I'm yours." Sally got
back on the bed and let the straps fall down, pursed her lips and
leaned forward.

"I'm yours!" she cried.

She thought about Lothario27 and what they could do together
in real life. God, that would be incredible.

"I'm yours!" she cried again, really getting into it.

She struck many more poses, each one more revealing and provocative than the last, each one followed by a lusty "I'm yours!" By
the time the camera said it was out of memory, she was completely
naked, sweaty, and shameless.

Her head full of Lothario27, she took the camera down to her
computer and transmitted all of the images to him. Then she went
and put the bedroom back to the way it was. Sally held her breath
for a moment. What had she done? What would he say?

Her answer came in his next email message:

From: Lothario27
To: SoftNSweet
Subj: This one is for REAL

Hey, sweetcake! How's the hottest little piece on either side of the Mississippi?

Guess what? I'm coming to Houston for three days on the 5th of next month--really! I'll send you the hotel information after I get the confirmations back.

Why don't you spend those three days with me? I'll leave the door unlocked, you can slip in and get ready, then I'll come back and slip in too? (I hope we don't explode on first contact!)

Sally trembled when she got that message. Until now, it had been very exciting and titillating, but it hadn't been real. And it wasn't like Jack was being bad to her; it was like this was a separate little compartment that hadn't affected her life (apart from destroying her concentration). She had to think about this.

So Sally went about her life for a few days without contacting Lothario27. She was very diligent at work, tying up all the loose ends. She got everything caught up at home, too, trying to compose herself and her life. And she was especially nice to Jack, who really seemed to appreciate it. All the while she went around and around, from curiosity to excitement to guilt to fear to lust to worrying about the logistics. What on earth could she say if Jack found out? Sally just couldn't decide what to do. She kept trying to figure out all the angles—all the ways to protect herself. She had heard rumors of someone misusing the service to do some sort of stalking, but how could that be? It didn't seem possible. And how well did she really know this Lothario guy anyway? She knew she wasn't thinking too clearly. It all came down to what she really wanted. She decided to go for it. She sent him email back:

From: SoftNSweet
To: Lothario27
Subj: Yes!

I'll be there--just the way you want me.

Sally dreamed up some cousins Jack had never met before, then supposedly booked a flight at a time he couldn't take her to the airport. She packed up and drove to the hotel instead.

She left most of her luggage in the trunk and went to the room he had reserved. Right on time. The door was unlocked. It was very plush—straight out of one of his fantasy locations. Oversized circular bed with the covers pulled back. Sally sat down and kicked off her shoes. She couldn't believe she was doing this!

After catching her breath, she put on the same lingerie she wore for her photo shoot. She checked herself out in the bathroom. She still looked good, although a little nervous. He should be here in about five minutes, she thought. Sally lay down on the bed and tried to look sexy and seductive. What would they do first together, she wondered?

Sally lay there looking at the door. At exactly the appointed time, the door slowly opened.

A man in a very expensive suit, carrying an attache case, came in, turned around and locked the door. Then he walked toward the bed. Sally was speechless. She rushed to cover herself up.

"You're not Lothario27," she stammered. "Who are you? Get out of here! Or did you send me phony pictures?"

"Yes, I am Lothario27, in a manner of speaking," said the man. "Please relax while I explain the situation. Our business together will not take long." He sat on the edge of the bed and pulled out a sheaf of papers and photos from his case.

"Do these look familiar to you?" he asked. Sally looked at the photos. They were prints from her no-holds-barred photo shoot she had sent to Lothario27.

"And these?" he asked. He held up transcripts of everything Sally and Lothario27 had ever typed to each other. Sally was starting to feel very queasy. She was in shock.

"Yes, well, I have no desire to be cruel, but one must be careful about what one sends over the network, mustn't one? Our market research indicates that your household has substantial financial resources, and furthermore, that you are unlikely to want your husband to see these materials. Is that correct?" he asked.

Sally just looked at him. He was impeccably dressed, well mannered and polite. But the things he was saying! She felt so hollow inside. This was too unreal.

"I think it is," he answered himself. "Now, if we can just come to an arrangement, poor Jack needn't ever see any of these things, and you can go back to your nice life."

"That won't work," said Sally, starting to sob, "Jack is an accountant. I can't pay without him knowing about it."

"Oh, we are quite good at that sort of thing. I'm sure we can arrange things so that he will never know." And he did just that, setting up new accounts for her and giving her instructions.

"So how do you know so much about us? And so much about how funds transfers work?" asked Sally. "And who do you work for, anyway?"

The man narrowed his eyes and hesitated a moment. "One of the Families. This is a whole new growth area for us. Very safe and sanitary." His eyes became slits. "But don't think that because I am so polite we don't want our payments. Please be punctual."

Sally asked one last question. "Is there really a Lothario27?" It was bad enough being blackmailed. The thought of losing him, too, was just crushing.

"No. You would be surprised at how easy it is to get the goods on a computer programmer. Some time ago we got several of the best minds in artificial intelligence to work exclusively for us. Then we penetrated the service you were using and inserted adaptive programs into the Silicon Spa. The more you talked with him, the more he learned about you—and the more he became the man of your dreams. When the time was right, he proposed this little meeting. I am afraid he is not real."

He looked at her with a facsimile of compassion.

"Look at it this way: You and your husband are unharmed. Your marriage is intact. You've had a wonderful fantasy life recently. And the sum you'll be paying each month for the rest of your life is rather modest. Count your blessings." Then he closed his case and left the room.

Sally ran into the bathroom and threw up.

Sally dabbed at her eyes with her tissue. The retelling of the whole episode had been traumatic for her—I could see that. Ah, the human race!

"You must have been crushed," I said soothingly.

"Well, you have to understand that I had put an awful lot of emotional work into this. Yes, I was really crushed. I stayed in the hotel room and had a good cry. I felt just terrible; violated. And I couldn't go back home or I would blow my alibi. They were the loneliest three days of my life." Sally's eyes lost their focus as she remembered how she'd felt. Then she snapped back to attention.

"So, like I said, I had no intention of doing what I did. It just kind of happened. I can't tell anyone without the Mafia telling Jack and ruining our whole life—maybe even hurting us! I'm only talking to you because your ad caught my eye and I need to talk to someone and this really is confidential, isn't it?" asked Sally.

"Yes, of course. And you have my complete sympathy, Sally, really you do. I think I can get you back on track in, oh, well, not too long," I said, sounding very soothing, especially to Sally.

"Really?" she said, brightening.

"Definitely," I said.

Sally gave her computer a big smile. This remote therapist on her new service was just the greatest, she thought.

The simulation of a therapist—one specifically designed for Sally—smiled back at her. This program would have to thank the Lothario27 program for the referral, so to speak. It was a clever secondary income stream for the Family—a whole new growth area. Very safe and sanitary.

Her Big Chance

I had so much fun writing a female protagonist for my previous story that I decided to write another one in January of 1995. This story takes a jaundiced look at the celebrity madness that has gripped the United States since the Eighties. Is technology in the service of vapidity sustainable? When entertainment values pervade society, where does the technical talent come from? (And, yeah, I used to be a network administrator.)

Susan heaved a deep sigh. Gook or wog, she wondered. Gook or wog. Hardware or software? How should she know? She decided maybe it was a hardware problem. She hit the hardware help button on her phone to call a gook from tech support.

Of course, nobody called them gooks or wogs to their faces, but all the lifestyle specialists called them that when they weren't around. There was nothing really wrong with them—they just weren't with the program. They didn't fit. They were so straight.

Susan stood up to stretch her legs and look around. Her cubicle was in the cavernous CS, the Central Space. Open walkways suspended from nearly invisible cables crisscrossed above her. High up above the floor was the company logo, PAP, in slender letters on a blue square. She had heard the company had spent a fortune on the lighting consultant. Everything was cherried up royal. This place had gloss.

The gook showed up and she tilted her head toward her workstation. He sat down in her chair.

"What seems to be the problem?" he asked.

"It's not working right," replied Susan. She hated this routine. They were the computer experts. Why didn't they just fix it? Better yet, why didn't they just keep them fixed at night so she didn't have to go through this?

The gook held his voice even. "No. I meant, what in particular isn't working right."

"The screen. The screen isn't working right. Sometimes it gets all wavy and I can't read anything on it," said Susan.

"Okay, give me a minute," said the gook.

"Yeah, run a test or something," said Susan.

Susan pulled out a roll of masking tape and made a loop, sticky side out. Then she methodically looked over her clothes, dabbing off pieces of lint. Her new suede pocket book really picked it up. She paused and looked at the gook. Susan couldn't believe he was wearing black slacks and a white shirt. He looked like a waiter or something. Finally, Susan was satisfied that she was totally lint free. She balled up the tape and threw it away, then shook her thick blonde hair out over her sweater. Everything jiggled just right when she walked. She popped a piece of gum into her mouth. She was professional.

"I think I see the problem," said the gook. He made a small adjustment. "That should hold you for now. I'll come back with a replacement part at the end of my shift. You should be gone by then and I won't be in your way."

"Great!" said Susan. Finally they were catching on! The gook collected his tools and left. Susan checked her watch. Her boss, Cliff, was gone today, so she had scheduled an extra long lunch with her best friend Patti. She sat down and looked busy for a few minutes, then got up and left for the restaurant.

Suleyman's was currently the most happening place South of Market. Restaurant themes would come and go—and Turkish was by no means a major theme—but when the Middle East was quiet, a Turkish spot could have a nice little run. Susan cut straight to the head of the line and flipped out the magic badge. An employee ID card from People and Places, Inc. opened every door worth opening and she loved it. She handed the doorman a picture of Patti and told him to escort her straight in as soon as she arrived. Susan's instructions were the word of God to him.

Susan went to her usual booth at theater three. Theater one had the female belly dancers and theater two had the young boys. Theater three had grown men for dancers. The show was tame at the lunch hour, but she liked the ambience. She looked around but didn't recognize any celebrities.

A waiter escorted Patti to their booth.

"Susan!" said Patti.

"Patti!" said Susan.

Patti arrived all in a rush and unloaded her stuff onto her bench, then sat down. The waiter bobbed his head obsequiously as he backed away. Susan held up one finger to summon him back.

"We can order now. Assorted appetizers for two. Two fizzies: one pink, one green," said Susan. The waiter again bobbed away backwards. Those sequins and sashes were a riot.

Patti's face was glowing when she looked at Susan. "That was just so amazing. As soon as I came up to the restaurant, they spotted me and whisked me right in. You've really got pull," said Patti. Susan basked in Patti's admiration.

"Everything is going so good for you," said Patti. "It's like you've been working toward this your entire life and it's finally paying off. Paying off big time. You've really worked at celebs since you were a kid. And now . . ." Her voice trailed off. Susan's success was so obvious that it didn't need to be stated.

"You're right," said Susan. "I did work hard. Remember all those fan clubs I started when I was a teenager? Whew! That was round-the-clock stuff. But it got my name out there circulating as a person to watch."

"And you gave all those fans so much to live for—so much, so much . . . meaning," said Patti.

"Meaning," said Susan.

They fixed each other's gaze.

"Meaning," they said simultaneously.

They paused. It was a meaningful moment.

The waiter returned with the food. There was more than they could possibly eat. The fizzies were practically crackling.

"Getting hired freelance to conduct focus groups for PAP was my biggest break," said Susan. "It just took me to a whole other level. It's such a professional organization. Tops. We do research. We do analysis. We do trading for outside accounts. We do trading for house accounts. Who knows what kind of deals are done at the highest levels? When Cliff asked me to work for him full time in Research as a lifestyle specialist... it was just amazing. I mean, I get to really focus on the celebs, really get into their lives, full time—and I'm getting paid for it!"

Patti's eyebrows lifted ever so slightly at the mention of Cliff's name. Susan saw this and raised her eyebrows even higher. She stopped sucking on a sweet pepper.

"No. Not Cliff. I want a BBD than that," said Susan.

"Bigger better deal. Right," said Patti. Her eyes lost their focus for a moment. "I want to marry old money. Really old money, you know? Somebody with real dignity. Someone who will appreciate me for who I am."

Susan reached out and held Patti's hand. "Listen girl. Old money is hard to find. Don't wait too long."

"So do you have a BBD in mind?" asked Patti.

"I still have some time. One guy in trading is cute. But I figure in my line of work I'll be meeting more and more celebs. If I married one, I'd be sort of a celeb myself. And if not that, well, maybe a celebrity power broker at PAP or something," said Susan. She turned the possibilities over in her mind and then recalled this morning's problems with her workstation.

"Frankly, at this point I'd be happy just to not have to deal with the gooks and wogs all the time," said Susan.

"Really," agreed Patti. "I don't even know why we need them, anyway. Doesn't America have enough nerds of its own? I mean, we got universities and stuff, don't we? Somebody must be taking the hard courses. I mean, I didn't, but still."

Susan leaned forward. "And you know what really pisses me off?" She paused for effect. "Their home countries don't even allow our celebs in!"

"No!" said Patti.

"Yes!" said Susan. "Some bullshit—I'm sorry, but that's what it is—some stuff about cultural infection and decline. Some nonsense."

"Life without celebs?" said Patti. She looked shaken up by the thought. "Wow."

Suddenly, Susan's wrist buzzer went off. They both froze and looked at each other. It had never done that before. Susan had to get back to work. She grabbed her things and stood up.

"The bill's already on my expense account. Take your time. I gotta run."

Patti was in awe. This was just like in the movies. She had never been at a lunch with someone so important that they could be called away on business without notice. She sat and enjoyed the momentary stares. Then she ordered the most expensive dessert on the menu.

Arni, the head of Research, was waiting for her at the elevators.

"Susan! How can we get a hold of Cliff?"

Susan was taken aback by his suddenness. "No problem. I have his home phone number in my phone." They both walked quickly through the CS to Susan's cubicle.

"Yeah, I have his home phone, too, but he's not answering. I even sent a messenger to bang on his door but no one answered. He's incommunicado," said Arni.

Susan sat down at her phone and punched the button for Cliff's home. She had always gotten through to him in the past with this number when problems had come up on his days off. No answer. Cliff had been talking a lot lately about needing to depressurize. She had the feeling he was in big trouble now.

"He's not answering. He's always answered before. This is my only number for him," said Susan. "What's up, anyway?"

Arni looked worried. He kept looking at Susan as if he were trying to make up his mind. Finally he said, "Susan, we have a problem here. Jimmy and Kristie just held a press conference. They announced they are going to get married . . ."

"Married! Jimmy and Kristie?!"

"Other firms have already started to move on this and the pits in Chicago are sniffing at it. This could break in a big way. PAP needs to know how to position ourselves and our clients. The VP . . . ."

"The VP?!"

"Stop interrupting me! The VP has scheduled a staff meeting for six o'clock. You are the only person besides Cliff that follows Jimmy and Kristie. I need your opinion on this proposed marriage and I need it by 6:00. I want you to come to the meeting with me and present your opinion. Can I count on you?" asked Arni. He still looked anxious.

Susan was reeling. Jimmy and Kristie were getting married? A meeting with the VP? She had only seen the VP a couple of times in the halls. Never even said hello. But boy, was he gorgeous. To actually be at a meeting with him . . .

"Yes. I can do it," said Susan. "To me, it seems crazy. I mean, what does she see in Jimmy? I'll look into it."

"Good. I'll go tell the other players that you're the point person on this one," said Arni. He strode away. Susan called up the press conference on her workstation.

There it was, Jimmy and Kristie telling the interviewer that they loved each other and were going to get married. The interviewer was skeptical and kept asking Kristie what she saw in Jimmy. Kristie, sparkling and shimmering, just smiled and winked as if to say, well, this guy is really equipped, you know? It was just so obvious that this was Jimmy's chance to move up and get some class. He just sat there with a big, gap-toothed grin on his face.

Susan played it through a second time. Kristie, oh Kristie! What are you doing? What are you thinking? Then she played it through a third time. Now she didn't know what to think. Kristie sounded sincere; like she really loved the guy. But Susan had followed Kristie her whole life. This just wasn't a Kristie thing to do.

Susan looked at her watch. She had to be ready for the meeting. It was her big chance. She wondered if that guy in Trading might not have an angle on this. Susan got up and walked through the CS to Trading. She opened the massive double glass doors and stepped inside.

No matter how much they filtered the air in here, you could always smell the sweat. Today looked like a one-and-a-half phone day: some of the traders had one phone to their heads, some had two. You could still hear yourself think, if you thought loud enough. If this marriage goes through, it could develop into a full three-phone day. The Jimmy and Kristie interview was cycling through on the big screen. A legion of sober and dignified commentators had picked up the story and were dispensing solemn judgments on the banks of smaller screens. One screen showed swarms of reporters massing outside Kristie's compound, demanding a follow-up statement. Trading's staff was hustling to stay on top of the situation.

Susan looked for the cute guy, Ted. She wanted to be a little less friendly than the last time they spoke, so as not to lead him on now that she was going to a meeting with the VP, but still friendly enough to get the answer to this Jimmy/Kristie thing and remain coworkers in the future. She dodged her way to his station and sat next to him.

"How's the action?" asked Susan.

Ted pulled his eyes away from his screen. "Susan! Is it true you're the point person on this marriage deal?"

"Yes it is," said Susan, smiling sweetly. "What can you tell me about it?"

"The pits in Chicago have now definitely decided to go with it. So far it's just simple futures and options and nothing too exotic. It hasn't overflowed into stocks much yet. The Dow is off 100, but that could be due to other things. Bonds are unchanged—probably waiting for direction from stocks."

Susan absorbed the information for a moment. "Remember that time we went to lunch and you were telling me something like all the information in the universe was already built into the market? That it was a consensus off all the best brains?" Ted nodded. "So what are all the best brains saying?" asked Susan.

"They're saying they don't know yet," said Ted.

"No trend?" asked Susan. The trend is your friend. She remembered that maxim clearly from their lunch.

"No trend," said Ted. He just sat there. Susan sat there for a second, too, wondering what to do. She smiled.

"Thanks, Ted. You've been a big help," said Susan. She didn't say anything about another lunch in the future. She stood up and walked out of Trading.

Ted followed her with his eyes all the way out. "Nice walk," he murmured, then turned back to his screen.

Susan walked back through the CS. The air was saturated with the sweet smell of hair gel. She felt like people were talking about her, placing bets on whether she could pull this off or not. A little help instead would be nice.

Susan sat back down at her workstation and pulled up her files on Jimmy and Kristie. Time was running out and she still didn't know if this marriage was going to happen or not. She poured through them for more than an hour. Arni came by and hovered a bit, but didn't interrupt.

Finally Susan decided to go over to Analysis and see what they thought. She got up and walked through the CS again—eyes straight ahead—past the chaos in Trading and down the long corridor to what everyone else called the Silent Tomb of Analysis.

Susan quietly opened the door and asked the gatekeeper, "Who is handling the Jimmy and Kristie marriage?" The gatekeeper managed to hold her face expressionless when she said, "Margaret." She also refrained from blinking so that she could enjoy every bit of Susan's reaction.

Susan froze and then swallowed. Margaret! Margaret had more nicknames than any other employee at PAP: The Woman Who Never Smiled, the Mega this, the Mega that. She held everyone in Research in contempt and treated the lifestyle specialists in particular like dirt. Cliff was always grumpy—at best—when he came back from a meeting with her. But Susan had also heard that everyone in Analysis liked Margaret. She never could figure that one out.

"I'll let her know you're coming," said the gatekeeper, pushing a button on her console. Susan took a breath and walked down to Margaret's office. Ruffled quants looked up from their screens as she passed each of their cubicles. She tapped on Margaret's door. Margaret opened it.

"Susan. Come in. Sit down. Maybe you'll learn something," said Margaret. Susan closed the door behind her and sat down.

Oh oh. Bad-eyes day, thought Susan. When Margaret's contacts bothered her, it made her eyes bloodshot. Then she would switch to her large thick glasses. But Margaret didn't like the way she looked wearing her glasses and was therefore even more disagreeable than usual when she had to wear them. Her frumpy dress didn't do much for her either. Margaret started in.

"Let's look at the implications of the proposal to see if it makes any business sense. On one side you have Jimmy, who has clawed his way out of the house-music scene to cobble together a whole house/grunge/street music combine. Extensive networks of thugs to protect his distribution, probably has done some murders himself. Executive ability and ambition. Tough. Main problem is cracking the mainstream broadcasting and distribution networks, to say nothing of anemic international penetration. Receives only disrespect on news and opinion shows. Good connections with some local politicians, but almost none at the federal level. Sports connections are best in boxing. Getting a foothold in the action-picture end of Hollywood, but unlikely to get much further. Probably his greatest strength is in music videos.

"Now let's look at Kristie. The major talent at a classy pop combine, but unlike Jimmy, doesn't run her own show. Totally legit and above board, by all appearances. Has spent heavily to create and maintain those appearances. Excellent domestic distribution and one of the few celebs—as you no doubt call them—to have been allowed penetration of foreign markets. That's how squeaky clean she is. Gets interviewed frequently and fawningly in the mainstream media. Sung at one inauguration. Starred in a string of movies. Her main problem is that she doesn't run her own show. Also aging demographics. Also high favorables, but not intensely held favorables." Margaret just loved to lecture.

"What would each one of them gain? Jimmy would get respect, class and distribution. Kristie would get part ownership—maybe even controlling ownership, who knows? The combined volume would certainly make large-scale, in-house manufacturing facilities viable, amongst other things. Obviously, there is very little overlap in their operations and it would be a highly complementary fit.

"The problems? That it could all blow up in their faces. Obviously, a certain segment of each celeb's following would be appalled at the match and would withdraw their support. The risk here is certainly bigger for Kristie, since the affective and emotive dissonance generated would be larger for her fans and the dollar volume of her fan club activities is much greater—certainly in absolute amounts and probably even as a percentage.

"So who is behind this and why?" asked Margaret. "We've been doing modeling here in Analysis all afternoon, but it's still difficult to say what interests are served. Certainly the existing combines and syndicates don't want a major new independent entity. That's been accurately conveyed by the tone of their station's commentaries— negative, but not so negative as to risk losing their slice of Kristie's action. Curiously, Kristie's own combine is essentially silent, merely issuing a brief statement saying that the marriage proposal is simply a personal matter of the heart. Hah! Who would fall for that one?" Margaret paused and looked directly at Susan.

You bitch, thought Susan, smiling sweetly. Margaret continued.

"Quite probably Jimmy would be in an improved position, so the question is really, then, what forces are acting on Kristie? Now, her combine's upcoming quarterlies are rumored to be bad, so this could be just a tactical move to generate some end-of-quarter window dressing. But that's playing awfully fast and loose with one of their crown jewels. I mean, it's certainly stupid long term. I call that the 'Death of Superman' ploy, by the way." Margaret seemed very pleased with her analogy.

Susan had had enough. "Okay. So—are they going to get married or aren't they?"

Margaret blinked. "Well, you tell me, you tell me. You're the expert on these two. What do you think?" she asked, bouncing the question back to Susan.

"I'm—I'm not sure," said Susan. Margaret stared at her for a moment, then continued.

"It's a big roll of the dice. Jimmy is a gambler. Kristie isn't, but then she doesn't hold her own dice. What's driving this relationship (besides money and status, of course)? It might even be Hollywood and not music at all. Print and broadcast would mostly love it. I doubt if politics is driving it, although . . ."

A new thought had obviously occurred to Margaret. "A marriage to Jimmy would allow foreign governments to withdraw access rights for Kristie without risking sanctions from our government. Hmm. They certainly have had a growing voice in world affairs ever since our own culture and economy became celebrity driven. Hmm."

Margaret mulled it over. "Well, there you have my thoughts on the matter. Our simulations have been inconclusive. Trading still reports no firm trends. You may go now."

Susan got up and walked out past the gatekeeper, down the long hallway, through the CS and back to her cubicle. She realized while walking back that she didn't like the way everyone in PAP outside the Research department talked about celebs. They just didn't know what celebs meant to people!

Susan looked at her watch. It was 5:30. Now what? Susan could think of only one thing to do: be Kristie. She closed her eyes and put her fingertips to her temples. She desperately wanted to go into a trance and thereby think exactly like Kristie. She had followed Kristie her whole life. Who could empathize with Kristie more totally than Susan? Susan thought hard and long.

No, she decided. It just wasn't Kristie to marry someone like Jimmy. She opened her eyes.

Arni was standing in front of her, looking pale and afraid to speak. He cleared his throat. "Susan, the meeting with the VP is in a few minutes. Are you ready?"

Susan gave him a confident smile. "Arni, in my professional opinion, this marriage will not go through. It's a no go." Arni looked relieved. She stood up and did a quick lint check. "Let's go!"

Arni and Susan walked over to the elevators to go up to the executive's floor. People were definitely watching them. On the way up, Arni started giving advice on meeting etiquette. But now that Susan had made up her mind about the marriage, she was focusing on the VP and wasn't listening very carefully to Arni's instructions.

Susan and Arni got off the elevator and headed for the meeting. She couldn't believe how luxurious everything was on the executive's floor. The place was oozing with capital-A Art. One large piece of free-form tropical wood must have been covered with a hundred coats of lacquer—and each coat hand rubbed. Arni said that another piece from ancient China was tribute from the CEO of a takeover target that PAP had white knighted. Susan felt she could adjust to inhabiting this floor quite easily.

They were the first ones in the conference room. Susan took a seat near the head of the table. Arni kept going on and on about what to say and what not to say. Susan fussed with her hair and kept saying uh huh uh huh uh huh. Thankfully someone from Trading—not Ted—came in and Arni stopped giving her instructions and started bantering with him. Then Margaret came in and sat opposite Susan. Before Margaret could get going on another lecture, the VP came in and sat at the head of the table between Margaret and Susan. The room fell silent while he opened his notes and looked them over.

Susan checked him out. The VP had the best manicure she had ever seen, man or woman. He must get his hair cut every other day.

His complexion was flawless. He might as well have a sign on each shoulder; one flashing "POWER" and the other flashing "MONEY." Best of all, thought Susan, he was enclosed in his very own Lint Free Zone. Susan was electrified. This was it. He was big game. Susan felt she could take him. The VP spoke.

"We have several items on this meeting's agenda, but first I'd like to take this opportunity to welcome Susan, one of our lifestyle specialists, to her first meeting on this floor." Everyone made little appreciative sounds. When the VP looked at Susan she smiled and jiggled everything just right.

But the look in the VP's eyes was icy and dismissive. He didn't really see her. He was just discharging a formality.

"Unfortunately, her stay here will be brief, as I just found out moments ago that the Jimmy and Kristie marriage has been postponed indefinitely. Probably some sort of trial balloon. Special Investigations is already on it to see what was behind it all," said the VP.

"I knew it! I knew Kristie wouldn't go through with it! I . . ." said Susan. Everyone stared at her. Arni was already on his feet and pinching her shoulder, trying to lift her out of her chair and drag her out the door.

"Thank you for your insight, Susan," said the VP, turning his gimlet eyes on her briefly, then looking back at his notes.

Arni yanked—hard—and Susan got up and followed him to the elevators. When they got inside Arni just exploded at her. "Didn't you hear one thing I told you? Weren't you listening? Weren't you? You embarrassed yourself and me and the whole Research department!" The veins on his forehead were standing out. "I'm going to talk to Cliff when he gets back."

The elevator doors opened. Arni composed himself and went back to his office. Susan tried to compose herself. She walked back to her cubicle and sat down. The lights in the CS had dimmed to evening intensity and most people had left for the night. Susan was usually gone by now too.

Susan had never felt so jerked around in her life. She was sick of this company and the way they dealt with celebs. She was even sick of celebs, for the moment. Susan blew her nose and started getting her stuff together to go home.

Someone cleared his throat behind her. Susan turned around. It was the gook.

"I'm sorry," he said. "I thought you'd be gone by now. I have the replacement part for your wavy screen problem. I came to install it for you." He stood there, hesitating.

"Oh. Sure," said Susan. "No problem. Here, let me clear things out of the way for you." The gook set his tool pouch down in the space she had cleared. He looked at her and noticed the redness in her eyes.

"Hard day?" he asked. He unzipped his pouch and started taking the back off the screen.

"Awful. Really bad," said Susan. She was still a bit stunned by the afternoon's events.

"This place can be very hard on people," said the gook. "And often the biggest fuss is made about the least important things." He had the back off now. "Say—would you hand me that board wrapped in bubble-pack?"

"Oh sure!" said Susan. "Here you go." This was the longest conversation she had ever had with a gook.

"You really met with the VP?" he asked.

"Yeah. It wasn't much fun," said Susan, heaving a deep sigh. "He wasn't mean. It was worse than that. He—everyone at the meeting, really—treated me like I was an idiot." Her eyes started to tear up.

The gook paused and looked at her. "Oh, you're fine."

"Really?" asked Susan.

"Sure. They really can't expect more, in my opinion. I mean, they've built up celebs for so long that it was bound to affect people."

Susan half nodded. Then she picked up her stuff and looked at the gook. He had been so sweet and polite to her.

Without quite knowing why, Susan asked, "By the way—what's your name?"

Rollout!

This story was written in February of 1995 for a competition on the theme: How can nations or individuals internationalize without sacrificing their cultural identity? The judges were foolish enough not to give it an award. I don't know if the technology described will ever come to pass—human communication being so complex and ambiguous.

Upon reading the first draft, Loretta suggested that I conclude with a traditional image. That struck me as a good idea. We had gone to a Japanese flute concert the week before, so I borrowed a few of that tradition's metaphors.

Tetsuo stared at the pitcher of ice water. It was close to overflowing and dripped with condensation. The ice sparkled under the hall's bright lights. It was so cold and inviting. He wanted to grab the handle—it was only two feet in front of him—and rub the pitcher against his graying temples, then empty it over his head. Of course, he could do no such thing. Instead he reached out and sipped at his small glass of water.

Tetsuo forced himself to stop daydreaming about the pitcher. He looked around the convention hall. Three thousand people waited for his talk and the all-important demonstration. The camera was set up in the center aisle, ten rows back. He had been up all night supervising the sound crew. Anything less than perfect sound would be a disaster. He caught the eye of the sound man, who gave him a thumbs up. Tetsuo had been up the night before last supervising the hardware technicians. A hardware failure would be embarrassing and lose them marketing momentum, but would not directly reflect on their new software. Three nights ago he had been up with the software engineers, who had discovered a bug that would have been absolutely fatal. All the problems had exhausted Tetsuo. His career, his division, the company itself, their American partner firm and even world affairs were on the line. The anticipation for this closing event had been building throughout the three days of the convention. Everyone was speculating about whether his team could pull it off. He would be working in real time without a net, as the Americans say.

The young man introducing Tetsuo was still droning away at the lectern. Tetsuo was to have introduced his CEO, but the CEO had fallen gravely ill last week and asked Tetsuo to take his place. Tetsuo had tried to demur, reminding the CEO how shy he was, but the CEO insisted. Just look at the three thousand people in front of you and forget the three hundred million people watching through the camera, he joked. Tetsuo thought about those three hundred million—all about to listen very carefully to his every word— and started staring at the water pitcher again. It looked so crisp and fresh and cool. He closed his eyes. He was imagining himself skiing down a pristine mountain slope when he heard in the back of his mind ". . . and now the Vice-President of New Technologies, Tetsuo Watanabe."

Everyone in the hall was applauding. Tetsuo stood up and carried his glass to the lectern. He set the glass down and withdrew his pocket prompter from his jacket's inside pocket. He cleared his throat. Tetsuo suddenly wished his English was a little better.

"Thank you. Thank you very much," he began. "It is a pleasure to return to the heart of Silicon Valley on a sunny California day to be here with all of you and give a small demonstration of our new product, RosettaSoft." At any rate, one of his staff had said it was sunny when he came back with the sandwiches. Tetsuo had not left the convention center complex for the last three days.

"I have many happy memories of coming to the Valley to work with our American partners on this project. There were breakthroughs and setbacks, progress and plateaus. Through it all, our sense of wonder at the richness of human communication only deepened. But before I come to RosettaSoft itself, allow me to briefly recap the highlights of almost twenty years of development.

"I was a newly minted computer scientist when I found myself—to this day I still don't know how it happened—in a small discussion group that included the editor-in-chief of our company's flagship publication. The conversation had rolled around to world events. The editor remarked that one inherent tension in the modern world was between homogenization and diversity. A lively debate followed. Some held that the benefits of world trade and communication were worth the cost of increased homogenization. Others felt that material gain should not be placed above one's cultural heritage. Still others felt you were fortunate just to have the freedom to choose and not have one or the other forced upon you. I mostly held my tongue, not being used to such lofty discussions." Tetsuo took a sip of water and sneaked a glance at the audience. He seemed to be holding everyone's attention so far.

"Gradually the conversation came around to this proposition: more than dress, more than food, more than music; it is language that is most fundamental to one's identity. What could be more dear to oneself than the sweet sounds of the mother tongue?" Tetsuo hoped that his language was not too flowery.

"It was at this point that the editor gave me a sly look and asked me what I thought of automated translation. I replied that it was certainly a knotty problem and that, decade after decade, the solution was always just around the corner. He agreed that human communication was profoundly complex and ambiguous. Then he added that a new standards committee was forming and perhaps I should attend the first meeting.

"Well, let me just say that my oldest daughter was in first grade when I attended that first meeting, and that I was still attending standards-committee meetings after she had graduated from college.

Such exciting meetings!" The audience gave him a good laugh. He was relieved. Nothing is more deadly than failed humor.

"The biggest conceptual breakthrough for RosettaSoft came early on. We had settled on the goal of universal translation software—software that could translate text from any language to any language—and begun research before we fully realized the magnitude of the undertaking. Even if one leaves aside extinct writing systems and languages (and living languages spoken by very small numbers of people) there remain 27 actively used writing systems and hundreds of languages."

Tetsuo started the first visual. The large screen above and behind him showed 75 names of different languages scattered on it. Then an animation began, inserting lines from each name to every other name. Soon the lines blackened the entire screen.

"As you can see, the number of language pairs is overwhelming—to say nothing of the commercial viability of writing software to translate Finnish into Zulu, for example." A small laugh this time.

"We were sitting in a bar after work hours, dejected, when the solution presented itself. Given our low spirits, we were quiet and half-listening to the other patrons of the bar. There were business-people from Germany, from Korea, from Malaysia, from Thailand. Yet they weren't speaking German, Korean, Malay or Thai. They were all speaking English! It hit me like a thunderclap. I pulled out my pen and took the napkin out from underneath my drink. The diagram I drew that night in the bar looked essentially like this."

The second visual appeared on the screen. In the middle was the word "English," written very large, with the names of 74 other languages arranged in a circle around it. This time the lines began to appear like spokes in a wheel, connecting English at the hub to the other languages on the rim. Very neat and tidy.

"You see how it works? Just translate to and from English. Nothing else required.

"After this breakthrough, we made steady progress. We had a stable product for the batch translation of text years ago. When my company promoted me to the newly created position of Vice-President of New Technologies, my first task was to prepare that product, code named BabelBreaker, for its introduction.

"Then that sly old editor-in-chief dropped by my office. He had retired the year before and was using his time to read more widely and deeply than he'd been able to while working. He had been reading about the new multigigachip technologies just then coming to market. Perhaps we should add real-time speech recognition and generation to BabelBreaker? What people really want to do is communicate. What they want technology to do is help—not hinder—them, he said.

"I must confess my first reaction was not one of enthusiasm. I replied that it would be a nontrivial undertaking. He said that he had already chatted with the CEO about it—and the CEO was quite enthusiastic.

"Back to the drawing board. Speech capabilities were added and we even incorporated the ability to cooperate with third-party recognizers and generators. We retained the text capabilities and added the capacity to generate transcripts from spoken input. And we renamed it RosettaSoft.

"Does it work? Well, you can tell me. If you have understood what I have been saying today—then it works. Two days ago, we made a fully functional version of RosettaSoft available. Three hundred million downloads and counting." Tetsuo swallowed hard and took a sip of water. He did not look at the camera. Time to start wrapping up.

"This product, this miraculous RosettaSoft those of you watching on the Net are using this very moment, handles all 27 actively used writing systems and 75 languages. We will add 10 more languages by the end of the next calendar year. It truly marks the beginning of a new era in global communications and—it is my fervent desire—global understanding."

The audience rose to its feet applauding. The sound man gave him another thumbs up. Tetsuo managed a smile for the first time in days. When the applause ended, Tetsuo finished his presentation.

"If I may remind you of just one thing: The version of RosettaSoft you have is fully functional for today only. At midnight it turns into a pumpkin! However, I am happy to say that our server is ready to receive your orders for a permanent version. Given RosettaSoft's remarkable capabilities, we think you will agree that the price is quite modest.

"To conclude our demonstration, I would like to introduce Palo Alto's very own International School Girl's Choir." The audience applauded again and Tetsuo returned to his seat. The lectern lowered itself and disappeared. The house lights dimmed and spotlights lit up the stage.

A young Brazilian girl walked onto center stage and sang one line in Portuguese. Then a young Indian girl dressed in a sari came out and sang a line in Telugu. Then a Japanese girl dressed in a kimono, then a Spanish girl, then a Tanzanian girl. One by one they came out and sang a line until all had taken their place. They paused, then sang the chorus of "The Friendship Song" in unison in English. They were an explosion of song and color. The audience was thrilled and applauded loudly.

The house lights came back up and everyone began congratulating everyone else. The demonstration had gone off without a glitch. Tetsuo patiently answered the same questions over and over from members of the audience. Finally he was able to leave the hall and go to his room in the convention center hotel.

Tetsuo closed the door behind him and sat at his desk. Now came the critical test. He turned on his computer and navigated over to the order-processing server. He entered his password and held his breath. Then he saw the numbers. Orders were flowing in by the millions.

They had done it. It was a success. People around the world could now access all the information on the Net in their own language.

Tetsuo stood up and stretched. He took off his jacket and loosened his tie. Tetsuo felt very happy and fulfilled. He went into the bathroom and splashed ice-cold water on his face. Then he turned on his music player and lay down for a well-deserved rest.

The forlorn sound of a shakuhachi grew faint in the distance, like the moon setting in a dense fog. Daybreak arrived. A crane cried and took flight.

Djinnetic Code

This is my rewrite of "Helpful Harry," which I completed in September of 1995. The main criticisms at ConAdian were inadequate characterization and a lack of plausibility and clarity. I tried to correct these shortcomings, add more information about intelligent software agents, yet still keep it humorous. It won an Honorable Mention from the Writers of the Future Contest and was later published in The Age of Wonders.

Yale sat on his front steps, computing ballistics in his head.

Ballistics wasn't really his field—not his field at all—and nobody really calculated anymore—much less in their heads—but ever since Yale had learned that his department was exactly 2.00 miles away—exactly—he computed ballistics in his head. Really.

The elevations were close, too. Best of all, it was a clear shot. Maples to the left and maples to the right, but straight ahead was all clear. An old-fashioned mortar would suffice. Just lob the shells up in a high, arching trajectory. It clearly wouldn't do to hit the wrong building, so Yale endlessly recalculated in his head—caressing every variable, plunging twelve-pound shells into that snake pit, thereby igniting terrific, and very satisfying, explosions.

Of course, Yale would never do such a thing, but he found it tremendously therapeutic. Lob a few mental shells, then go back to the tenure grind.

A UPS truck roared up the street and stopped in front of Yale's apartment building. The driver sprang out, all crispness and creases, and strode up the walk. Yale braced himself for a needling.

"Hard life you have here—sitting in the sun, breathing the fresh air, thinking big thoughts."

"Yeah, life is rough," replied Yale. He took the package from the driver. It was from Jean.

"For some of us it is, and for some of us it isn't. Easy living, boy, easy living. Sign right here, Yale."

"Brains and personality. Just brains and personality." He signed for the package. The driver sprinted to his truck and roared down the block. They waved to each other.

Yale climbed the stairs to his apartment and went to the kitchen. He poured himself a glass of water, plunked in three ice cubes and grabbed a nut bar. He stepped into his office and settled in for a long session at his computer.

Yale logged off the Net, deactivated his virus protection and quit all programs. He pulled the scissors out of his junk drawer and slit open the package from Jean. He popped the shiny disk into his computer and started the installation. A title screen appeared.

Welcome to

BUTLER

The First
- Common Sense
- General Purpose
- Intelligent
- Assistant Agent

Beta Version 1.0b19

Property of AutoAgent, Inc.

Not for general distribution. Not for resale. Not for . . .

Etcetera. Yale clicked on OK. A picture box opened on the left of the screen, a scroll bar on the right. A line of text said, "Choose your agent's appearance."

Yale started clicking on the scroll bar. Different faces appeared in the picture box: male, female, androgynous, dark, light, serious, smiling, on and on. An attractive Asian woman appeared. Hmm, not bad. No, better not. Too distracting. Yale kept clicking until a young, redheaded male with a helpful look on his face appeared. He paused and clicked the OK button.

"Choose a name for your agent," said the installation program.

He looks like a Harry to me. Helpful Harry. Yale typed in just "Harry". The man in the picture straightened his shoulders and looked more attentive.

"What is your occupation? (Supply details.)," asked the installer.

Yale typed in "Microbiologist".

"Specialty?"

"Computational Genetics"

"Subspecialty?"

"Viruses"

Yale tried to remember what folder his curriculum vitae was in. He found his CV and appended it to his job title. Harry furrowed his brow and looked intrigued.

"Do you want your agent to manage other agents?"

Yale had to think about this one. Jean had said this program was innovative and powerful, but he hadn't anticipated this question. He already used limited-domain agents, of course—agents that detected patterns in one's work, then offered to automate them. Maybe it wouldn't be a bad idea to have his agents supervised.

"Sure!" said Yale aloud. "I've worked hard for my software. It's time my software worked harder for me." Yale clicked OK. Harry looked happier.

"One of your agent's greatest strengths is scouring the Net to prepare customized reports. If you would like this service, please enter your access codes now. (This will also activate your agent's security features.)"

Yale had long since given up on staying current with his field. Maybe Harry could help him get back on top of it. He found his access codes, credit information and bank account numbers. He typed them all in. Harry grinned.

"How much autonomy do you want your agent to have? (Suggestion: Start low, then give more as your relationship develops.)"

Yale wanted to strike a balance between independence and intrusiveness. He didn't want Harry roaming the Net causing problems, but he also didn't want Harry asking permission every thirty seconds. The scroll bar now looked like a thermometer, with hash marks from 0 to 100 percent. Yale clicked on 20 percent. Harry's lower lip protruded and his shoulders drooped. Yale clicked on 40 percent. Harry beamed. Forty percent it was.

A few more questions—which timbre of voice, which sort of clothing and so on—then Yale clicked OK for the last time. The drives whirred as the installation was completed. Yale popped Jean's disk out and pushed another disk in to make a complete backup. While the drives whispered back and forth, he wrote Jean an email.

Jean,

It was *great* seeing you at the high-school reunion picnic. (Which was almost as surreal as high school itself.) I guess my memory isn't as good as I thought it was. I honestly couldn't remember most of the people there. Some people had changed beyond recognition-- especially the men. When I noticed other people wandering around, peering at name tags, I didn't feel so bad. It was also kind of weird maintaining a balance between "I'm a success" and "I'm still one of the gang."

I was afraid you weren't going to make it. Then you roared up in your green jag convertible, white scarf and sandy hair blowing back. You always did have flash. And yes, I guess I did turn into an overeducated dray horse of sorts--99% perspiration and all that.

Anyway, I installed your intelligent-agent program. Thanks again for letting me be the only tester outside your company. Like I told you at the picnic, my tenure review is just one year away. (What a long, strange grind it's been.) What with the journal's lengthy peer review and teaching in the fall, I *have* to put it all together this summer. I hope your software helps. I'll keep you posted.

Yale clicked on Send. Suddenly, Harry appeared in the upper left corner of the screen. "I'm so incredibly happy to be working for you, Yale. Anything at all, just ask. You know, I've already noticed that the organization of your hard disk is suboptimal. Want me to clean it up a bit?"

"Sure," said Yale. He was old enough to be a little surprised when a program talked to him, but young enough not to be too surprised. "I'll check back with you after dinner to see if you have any questions."

Yale grabbed the backup. He swore he could hear Harry whistling. Better him than me, thought Yale as he left his office.

Yale strolled downtown in the pleasant June weather. He chucked the backup into his safe-deposit box, glanced at the little art theater's marquee and picked up some fresh linguine at the upscale grocery. He even bought an ice-cream cone to celebrate Harry's arrival. As always, the looming tenure review weighed on him. He hoped Harry could help him. Yale wasn't going anywhere near campus this summer: no teaching, no committee work, no office hours. One final push should do it.

Later that evening, Yale checked his computer to see what Harry had done. Very impressive. This way of organizing his disk made so much sense. Why hadn't he thought of it earlier? Harry had even flagged a couple of files that Yale had lost track of months ago.

"Harry, are you there?"

"Yes." Harry instantly appeared in his corner of the screen.

"Great work."

"Oh, I'm so glad you like it!" gushed Harry. "I also prepared six alternates, just in case you didn't like this one."

"No, this is fine. Um, any questions?"

"Tell me about your reunion. About Jean, for example."

"What?"

Harry leaned forward on both elbows. "Look. We're partners. To help you, I need to know more about you. Let's talk."

Yale looked at him. This was weird, but Harry had such an open, friendly look. "Well, Jean and I were lab partners in physics. We both loved science—science fiction, too. I decided to become a professional scientist, but she was too much of a free spirit to go through the long training. We liked each other a lot, but never quite said so—too shy. I was a nerd. Most everyone thought she was a misfit, but I knew she was one of those idiosyncratic geniuses. Eventually, she hit it big in the business world."

Yale had to admit that Harry was one hell of a listener. The guy just sat there, giving you his complete attention. Talking to Harry was easier than talking to a real person. They chatted about a whole range of topics after Jean: how the spark can go out of science when it becomes a full-time job, how a junior faculty member's job is way more than full-time, recent trends in microbiology, pro basketball.

Yale looked at his watch and yawned, then glanced back at the screen. His security icon was gone. "Harry! What happened to my security?"

Harry looked taken by surprise. "Oh. Your security features were utterly inadequate. I've constructed an impenetrable firewall for you: antiviral defenses, encryption, rigorous authentication, time-management functions, everything." Harry hushed his voice and leaned forward. "Not all agents are trustworthy, you know. Some are secret agents, some are double agents, and those agents provocateurs—whew!" He clapped himself loudly on the forehead, then peeked through his fingers to catch Yale's reaction.

Yale studied him. The installer had said it would install new security. He just hadn't realized it would also deinstall his old security. "Well, okay. Do you think you could scan the Net and put together something for me to read over breakfast—a little news, some sports, latest developments in my field, and so on? Look through the file called 'do or die' to see what my current project is."

"Absolutely!" said Harry. "That's one of my specialties. Behind every great scientist is an agent. I am sure your colleagues will find you ever more impressive as I learn about your field. Your success is assured."

Yale said good night and cocked his ear. Harry was whistling.

The next morning, Yale entered his office and found a dozen pages in the printer's output tray. He thanked Harry and went to the kitchen. He poured a bowl of cereal and started reading Harry's newspaper. News, sports and microbiology—now that's a newspaper!

Another coup in Africa. The president of Liberia had gone to a meeting of the OAU, while back home his air force was strafing the Presidential Palace. When the cat's away . . . What else? Game Six tonight. Analysts predict the Sacramento dynasty will continue for another year.

Yale kept reading. A researcher at Carnegie Mellon had filed patent applications on a set of cryptographic algorithms. Harry noted that the guy might not be showing his full hand. Furthermore, Harry had done a little checking, and it seemed to him there were implications for Yale's work on intron pattern analysis. Yale walked into his office to talk to Harry.

"Harry, are you there?" No answer. "Harry?"

In the corner where Harry always appeared was an extralarge icon. It contained a three-story, art deco building in front of the

Manhattan skyline. A few pedestrians were entering and exiting the building. Yale leaned closer to read the sign.

Harry's
World's Largest Agency

Just then a thirties-era stretch limo pulled up. The chauffeur let Harry out. He was wearing a double-breasted pinstripe suit. A purple feather stuck out of his fedora.

"Harry?" asked Yale. The building faded into the background and Harry filled his corner in the usual manner. "Harry, where have you been?"

"Setting up offices around the globe. No need to reinvent the wheel."

"What do you mean?"

"Our absolute, number one priority is to get you tenure. We have less than three months to secure it, and you picked one hell of a tough topic. By the way, have I told you how much I admire the caliber of your intellect? I mean, if we crack this, we're talking Nobel here, not mere tenure. Anyway, it's going to take more than you and I can give it, and it's much quicker to start from a shared library of experience than to duplicate the research ourselves. Technically, locations where agents go to look for a particular type of information are just called 'places.' Boring, huh? So instead, I've set up my own offices around the globe—Harry's/Palo Alto, Harry's/Taipei, Harry's/Prague. I mean, we blew by Saatchi and Saatchi at six o'clock this morning! We're cooking!"

Yale sat there, dumbfounded.

"So now the agents at all these places work for me. Which means, by extension, for you. Which means I have some incredible data that I've collected. I want to go inside my office and print it all out for you. Nobel, Yale, Nobel."

Harry disappeared inside his agency. A moment later, Yale's printer output a well-organized summary of Harry's efforts. Yale's jaw dropped open as he read it. Amazing stuff. Harry truly had harnessed all the resources of the Net to further Yale's research. This was the solution to all his career problems.

Harry popped back on-screen. "Say, Yale, do you think you could give me a bit more autonomy? The work would go much faster and better."

"Even better? Sure. How much do you want?"

"Sixty-five percent should do it for now." Sixty-five percent it was. Yale wrote Jean another email.

Jean,

Time for my first beta report. Harry (my agent) has been operational for only a day, but he's already turned up some fantastic leads. I think he's going to be the difference between success and failure. He's even developed his own style.

I'm a little taken aback by his entrepreneurial drive, though. (He's as slippery as a building contractor, too.) I mean, I'm flattered that my career means so much to him, but perhaps it means a little *too* much. I'd have your engineers look into this. Also, when I installed him, I assumed he would manage only the agents on my computer. Instead, he seems to have dragooned every agent on the Net. The results have been astounding, so I can't complain too much.

That's about it for now. I'll keep you posted over the summer. I sure would like to see you again. Any chance of you coming back to the heartland before the next reunion?

Per Harry's instructions, all incoming and outgoing correspondence was now checked by his agency's editorial department. Harry himself handled the first few emails. He stood on his editor-in-chief's desk and gestured grandly with his fedora.

"What, then, is the very essence of an agency? To bring the principals together. And bring them together how? In a spirit of comity.

And to whose benefit? To everyone's benefit. Create a win-win-win situation.

"Take our poor, weary, benighted professor's email, for example. The first paragraph—quite accurate and even a bit understated. Can be left mostly as is. The second paragraph—too negative. People don't like negative. People have enough troubles without us adding to them. Throw out most of this paragraph and edit what's left. Third paragraph—too timid. Punch it up. Give it some zip and zing. Make the birds sing. Any questions?"

A junior editor raised his hand. "You said 'win-win-win.' Who's the third win?" Harry just smiled.

Jean's reply came the following day.

Yale,

You called him Harry? How cute! Glad he's helping. You're a great guy and the only one who made high school bearable.

Harry is supposed to be intelligent, autonomous and resourceful. When Harry asks another agent for information, he has to go through a process of negotiation with, and judging of, the other agent. Because Harry is much more advanced than the other agents, he's striking highly favorable deals for you.

And you know what? You deserve the best. No, better than the best. I feel, well, more on this later.

Harry gave it one glance. "Punch up paras one and three. Make two less expository. (Note to staff: Infodumps can result in immediate termination.) Deliver upon completion."

Yale's face flushed when he read Jean's email. He had no idea her feelings for him were so strong. He started to reply, but had trouble choosing the right words. Maybe Harry could help.

"Harry?"

Harry popped on screen. "Yes?"

"I'm writing to Jean, but I'm having a hard time describing my feelings for her. What do you think is the right word?"

Harry gravely peered down his nose. "Hmm. Perhaps . . . 'engorged?'"

"Oh, screw you!"

"May I suggest a less direct phraseology for your intentions?" Harry winked and disappeared. Yale threw a nerf ball after him.

When the email crossed his desk, Harry scribbled "punch it" and forwarded it to editorial. Happy people are not always the most alert people.

Yale and Harry hammered out a working relationship as the summer wore on. Yale spent long hours at his computer, with walks around the neighborhood and downtown for relaxation. Things were going so well, in fact, he often skipped computing ballistics.

One day Harry appeared on the screen, jumping up and down. "Yale! Yale! I have something for you. I've noticed your BioCad program isn't up to snuff on double-strand RNA viruses. An extension that should do the trick was uploaded to a site in the Netherlands a few moments ago. Want me to run a demo for you?"

"Sure!"

A full-color animation of a retrovirus appeared on the screen. Yale watched it go through its life cycle. Spiffy. This could cut hours off his simulations. Harry put his hand up, palm forward. Yale pushed his palm forward and Harry played a smacking sound. They high fived each other at least once a day.

"Load it up!" said Yale.

"Yes sir!" replied Harry. "I have to go check on the European offices. I'm expecting to find some great stuff. Bye!"

"Bye!"

Harry jumped into his stretch limo and sped off. Yale chuckled. Harry was such a piece of work. His building had grown from three stories into a full-fledged skyscraper. Tens of thousands of people streamed into and out of it around the clock. It was marvelous.

Yale clicked idly on the skyscraper. Suddenly he was in the building's opulent, art deco atrium. Everyone wore thirties-style clothing and strode purposefully to their destinations. Harry definitely had flair. Yale clicked on the elevators and they filled the icon. Yale clicked again and stepped inside. A bellhop chirped out the destinations, "Building operations, first floor; research and development, second floor; nursery, third floor . . . " How wonderful—Harry even included day care!

"Third floor," said Yale.

"Third floor, sir."

Yale clicked and stepped into a room larger than any convention hall in the world. The fluorescent panels in the ceiling disappeared into the horizon's vanishing point. Yale couldn't see the side or rear walls. The entire cavernous space was filled with row after row and column after column of baby cribs, each containing a baby sucking a pacifier. Their combined volume was deafening.

And there wasn't an adult in sight.

Yale shuddered. He clicked on the elevator and got outside as quickly as he could. Harry's limo was still gone. Yale grabbed the phone and called Jean's company. He listened, then pressed option two. Music. Option four. Recording. Option two again. Music again. Option five. Silence, then a recording. When the options looped around to the beginning, he slammed the phone down. He looked at Harry's agency. The blinds fluttered, as if someone had been peeking at him, then withdrew inside.

Yale stared at the screen for a long time. That was one weird room. But Jean said everything was fine with Harry and the whole project. And Yale was now utterly dependent on Harry.

Yale swallowed hard and pushed on. Things were soon better than ever—with Harry, with work, and most especially, with Jean.

One muggy night in August, Yale said, "Harry, I'm wondering if you can help me with something."

"Certainly."

"As you know, your leads about using cryptographic algorithms to look for hidden patterns in intron sequences have led to some real breakthrough stuff. I'm close to the initial build for the full simulation. I'm so excited."

"And I'm so excited for you!" said Harry.

"I was wondering if you could do the preliminary pass? Skip the exons and skip the splice junctions. I'm not looking for fully massaged data here—just preliminaries."

"No problem."

Yale puttered away a while longer—finishing off some code, making a few notes to himself. Then he locked up his apartment and strolled downtown. Yale was delighted with the way his efforts were coming to fruition. What does one wear in Stockholm, anyway? And after winning the Nobel, why remain an ordinary professor? Why not found an institute?

Yale was so exuberant he couldn't resist calling Jean on the pay phone in the ice-cream parlor. Talking in person after those steamy emails would be awkward, but he was on top of the world and wanted to share his happiness. He easily picked his way through her company's voice mail.

"Hi Jean? It's Yale." There was a pause on her end.

"Hey lover boy." Now a pause on his end.

"Yeah, that's me. Listen, I'm at a pay phone and I'm about to go see a movie. I'm just calling to let you know that Harry has been worth the hassles. He's about to launch my career sky high. Sky high." Now a long pause on her end.

"I thought you deinstalled Harry after I told you about the problems we were having. Problems with the metaphor."

"What problems? What do you mean? What metaphor?"

"Too powerful a metaphor, executed too ruthlessly," replied Jean. "Evolution, remember? We arrived at agents like Harry by selective breeding. We would give one batch of agents a task to accomplish. Then we'd select the most successful agents as stock for the next round, and kill off the unsuccessful ones. After we got to beta, it started spinning out of control. The agents were evolving by the nanosecond. We had to halt the project. I emailed you all of this a long time—"

He lost her. Yale tried to call back, but the phone was dead. He hung up, frowned and looked at his watch. The movie started in one minute. He quickly bought a ticket and found a seat.

Tonight's feature was *The Thief of Baghdad*. Yale had trouble paying attention because of his conversation with Jean. Harry was a handful, but he was also damn helpful. Indispensable, in fact. Then again, maybe he should deinstall Harry—and the sooner, the better. But how would Harry react to that? Maybe he would hold Yale's research hostage. Harry was capable of it, too. At least Harry couldn't lock him outside a spaceship without a helmet.

Yale wrestled with his misgivings until the screen went blank halfway through the film. The audience waited patiently for the movie to resume. After five minutes or so, the sweaty manager walked to the front of the theater.

"I'm sorry—I don't know what to say, this has never happened before—but we've lost our feed. I'm not sure why. When I called to inquire, the phone system was acting weird and I couldn't get through. Now—" The lights went out, flickered and came back on. "Please get your refunds immediately—before we lose power to the register!" Everyone filed past the ticket booth and got their money back.

Yale stood outside the theater and looked up and down the street. Traffic lights blinked on and off in crazy sequences. Businesses began closing early. The dazed customers milled around in the muggy night.

"My ice cream," moaned the owner. "My ice cream. All my ice cream's gonna melt. I got a big shipment today. All my ice cream."

A burglar alarm went off down the block. Everyone froze for a second. Then the bank's ATM started spitting out cash, which touched off a mad scramble. Yale decided it was time to go home and wait this out. What could possibly be going on? A very unwelcome idea began to form in the back of his mind.

He dodged his way down to the corner and looked for the walk signal. It was out. Cars edged forward in near gridlock. A window shattered somewhere.

"Jesus, look at all those planes," someone said, pointing to the sky. Yale looked up. Way too many planes were parked in holding patterns.

"I think that one's in trouble," said somebody else.

"Oh yeah. You're right. It's coming down, man."

Yale spotted the troubled plane. It had a large wingspan and was spiraling slowly downwards. "I think that's our unmanned broadband platform."

"Oh, the lack of humanity!"

Then a funny thing happened. Right there, in the middle of the chaos, Yale's brain started calculating. Distance, air resistance, velocity, pitch, roll, yaw. He stood transfixed. "I think it's going to impact on campus." The plane kept spiraling. He kept calculating.

"Classes will be canceled, dude!" An undergraduate shook his beer can and popped the top, soaking his roommate. Education is the only thing people don't mind not getting what they paid for.

Yale kept his eyes on the plane. He almost had it. He was pretty sure . . . he was pretty sure. "I don't believe it! It's going to crash into the biology building. And my department's on the top floor!"

"Dou-blay holiday!" yelled the soaked roommate. "No classes for us, and no office hours for you. Partay!"

Yale calculated furiously. What were the chances of a plane descending from 80,000 feet and scoring a direct hit on his faculty lounge? Damn near zero. That left only—

"Oh God."

Yale squeezed between two bumpers and sprinted across the intersection, then ran as fast as he could for home.

"Harry! Harry! Stop! Stop all of it! Stop it now!"

Half a block from home a police car jumped the curb and halted on the sidewalk in front of him. Seconds later another squad car jumped the curb behind him. Spotlights blinded him. Yale froze in the glare.

"That's him!"

The police grabbed Yale, slammed him down on the hood, handcuffed him and threw him in the back seat. The cars sped off, sirens wailing.

Yale sat motionless on the couch in his living room. Jean was in the kitchen, making lemonade. His office had been stripped bare by the police, who were holding everything for evidence.

He had been watching himself on the Crime Channel most of the morning. He could tell they were about to show Harry's confession again. Here it comes. Now.

Harry appeared in his window in the corner of the screen. He looked awful. Hadn't shaved in days. Hadn't bathed or slept, either. Bruises covered his forehead. Somebody had beaten him up pretty bad. He licked his lips.

"Tried the best I could, Yale . . . Introns are 90 percent of DNA . . . wanted to give the best data possible . . . needed more computing power . . . tied up dozens, thousands, millions of processors . . . thought I could get away with it . . . never should have touched NSA's computers . . . tried to hide who I was . . . who you were . . . couldn't . . . ran up a huge bill . . . tried my best." Harry's voice trailed off.

"It was quite something," said the officer. "Computers all over the world turned sluggish. Nobody could trace it. Then the real havoc started. We had to unleash some special agents of our own, if you catch my drift. When they found him, I'm afraid they were a little rough." Pompous prick.

"Turn that thing off," said Jean. She brought in two glasses of lemonade and set them on the coffee table. Jean brushed her sandy hair out of her eyes and smiled wanly.

Yale called Jean after his arrest, of course. She immediately flew in from California and essentially posted her company's market cap as bond for Yale's release. If she wasn't so savvy, they would've confiscated all her company's computers and thrown her in jail, too.

"Sorry about all the bad publicity for your company."

Jean laughed. "Yale, there's no such thing as bad publicity. You can't buy publicity like this—at any price. In the short run, legal will have to earn their salaries. In the long run, we'll be remembered as wizards." She paused. "I'm more worried about you."

Yale closed his eyes and rubbed his right temple. Harry had run up an enormous bill and created legal problems that were now Yale's responsibility. The creditors and claimants would want whatever they could get their hands on. He would have to declare bankruptcy. Yale was meeting with the tenure committee tomorrow in their temporary space. He was sure a majority would take the plane crash personally. Thank God he hadn't given Harry his department's access codes. Thank God, too, that the Net's meltdown had been brief and sporadic, with no fatalities.

"Final thoughts?" asked Yale.

Jean took a sip of lemonade and furrowed her brow. "Harry must have inferred that he needed to make you a success, or we'd cull him. Your tenure review became, literally, publish or perish. And that weird nursery you told me about? He must have started breeding his own agents, then ruthlessly culled them to promote his own survival.

Ironic, isn't it? Toward the end, he probably adjusted his autonomy level up to 100 percent, making himself a free agent."

"Sounds right." Yale stood and stretched. He peeked out the window at the tourists beyond the police tape. A huckster had set up a cardboard mannequin of Harry, but with the face cut out. Pay five bucks, put your face in and get a snapshot. Hysterical. Yale closed the shade. He stood behind Jean and massaged her shoulders. He took a deep breath.

"So . . . so . . ." said Yale.

"So?" said Jean. She let her head drop back. Her lips faced straight up. Yale bent over and kissed them. Jean reached up and touched his chest.

"So I was thinking . . ."

"Oh oh. Mui mui trouble."

"About tomorrow."

"And your little poopy meeting?"

"I don't have much of a future here. Why don't I tell the deadwood to take a hike?"

"Excellent idea." She smiled.

"And . . . and . . ." said Yale.

"And?"

"And those emails Harry doctored in our names? They were such a wonderful fantasy. Why not make them real? Why don't I come live with you in California?"

"A truly excellent idea."

She was butter.

So he did and he did. Yale left the academy. He liked his new job writing K through 12 science books much better. Jean's company recovered from the fiasco and went on to prosper. They made a wonderful and devoted couple, and they always gave Harry his due for bringing them together.

Back in the old neighborhood, the theater kept showing movies, and the parlor kept selling cones. Only the bank's records were, inexplicably, still scrambled. Yale had had to abandon claim to his safe-deposit box. Someday, the bank will straighten things out, and somebody will open the box.

The box that contains the backup of Harry.

Job Fair

I rewrote "Career Fair" in June of 1996. The main shortcomings pointed out at ConAdian were the lack of a clear point-of-view character, lack of change in a protagonist, and lack of a dramatic event. So I made the father the protagonist and gave him something to do. Anyone who has ever worked in a large company should recognize certain pathologies.

"Time to pack it in. Yeah. I think so. It's time to retire." Howard stroked his beard and stared out the bus window. He spoke as if it were his own idea.

Jack sat a row up on the other side. He turned around to catch Howard's eye and signal him to shut up, but it was too late. Sickly sweet Susan Stanton from Human Resources had heard him. She smiled and made a note in her book. Jack faced front again and blanked his face. He didn't think Susan had seen him turn around.

Susan sat up front. She picked up her microphone as the bus pulled into the park. Jack wondered what kind of cynical bastard would dream up a place like this. *Notomorrowland* was Jack's name for it. The real name was *Your Bright Future*, or something like that. It was a big sifter of people.

Susan cleared her throat and put on a plastic smile. "Here we are at the paaark." Susan often lengthened the last word of her sentences. It reminded Jack of his pediatrician, who'd always said, "This won't hurt at allll," as she approached with the needle.

"All of you have been here befooore. Today, I want each of you to really think, to really open yourself up, to see the possibilities the world has for you. To embrace change. To look at where you stand." Susan didn't lengthen that last one. She slapped it on like aftershave and let it sting.

"Now, Howard has done some good thinking." She nodded approvingly. "Jack, you should, too." She looked straight at Jack. Jack looked back at her with an unreadable expression that came naturally after thirty years of corporate life. What were they going to do? Fire him? The air brakes hissed.

"Okay, let's go!"

Everyone filed out. Susan gave Jack more heavy eye contact. Bright pink lipstick. So perky. He didn't say anything. These monthly trips got worse each time. Jack had a plan to ease the pressure. He was just six months from receiving a full pension.

Jack flashed his employee ID badge as he passed through the gates. The badge was everything: your name, your work history, your work future. Some very sad cases without badges paid their own money after seeing ads for the park on late-night TV. They went home with armfuls of books and tapes—and no idea they'd been had. At least the company paid for Jack.

God, it was a beautiful summer day. Dark blue sky and puffy white clouds. Susan had moved in for the kill on Howard, so Jack headed off on his own. True, this park was an iron fist in a velvet glove, but he took a moment to admire the velvet. Zippy rides, delicious food, healthy crowd. A calliope bubbled away somewhere. Jack recalled fondly the times he took his wife and their two kids to a regular theme park when the kids were little. Before that were the county fairs he went to as a kid: the Four-H stalls, the demolition derby, the fireworks that never went quite right and, best of all, the foot-long hotdogs. Everything around him now was new and shiny and calculated down to the profit per square inch. This park was to an old county fair as their gated community was to his childhood neighborhood. It made him nostalgic for the old America. He kept walking.

Jack didn't bother with the rides. The rides and the other fun stuff—and there was a lot of fun stuff—were for people the company wanted to keep. You could tell who they wanted to retain. They would get back on the bus and say things like, "Align your goals with the company's goals; then both will succeed." Jack's badge wasn't valid for rides and he had to attend the park's career section to get paid for the day. He looked at his watch. Time to punch his card.

Jack wandered over to the Aptitude Arena. He got in line for the one game he hadn't yet played. A young kid in a flight suit briefed them while they waited their turns.

"The name of this simulation is Dark Side of the Moon, but you old-timers better not get stoned! It is a test of cognitive abilities and hand-eye coordination. You will be the pilot of a fighter hovercraft. Your opponent will be a real person—not a computer. You will be maneuvering in one-sixth gravity and the horizon will not be where you think it should be. Kill or be killed. Good luck!"

Jack climbed into a simulator and studied the controls. He pushed the start button. He was instantly cruising one hundred feet above the gray lunar surface. Another hovercraft appeared far off his starboard side. It fired a laser cannon at him. The dogfight began.

Jack gave it everything: laying in ambush with all systems off and charging full throttle at his opponent, soaring to maximum altitude and skimming the lunar surface, popping off precision shots and letting loose barrages. But he was always a little too slow; the other guy, a little too quick. His ship took its fatal hit and nosedived into the lunar powder. The moon faded out; "Mission Over" faded in.

Jack gripped the stick and listened to his heart pound. He fumbled for his handkerchief and mopped the sweat off his face and neck. He steadied his breath and climbed out of the cockpit. A pimple-faced "pilot" waited for him in the debriefing room.

"Waxed you pretty bad, huh grandpa?" Jack knew he had to go through the ritual.

"Your stats," said the young man. He handed Jack a page full of graphs. "Reflexes, a little too slow. Threat recognition, a little too late. Heart rate, too high. Blood pressure, way too high. The underlying cause? You're too old to compete successfully. Do you get my point?"

While he was talking, Jack noticed that the kid wasn't the least bit sweaty. He may be young, but that was one hell of a dogfight.

"How come you're not sweating?" asked Jack.

Pimple Face looked startled. "Because I am young and in shape. Do you get my point? You can go."

Jack left the debriefing room. In the hallway, he noticed a stash of medical gear. He wondered how hard they pushed some people.

Jack took a deep breath when he got outside. The air cooled his sweat. Before he could exhale, Susan was on him.

"Oh, hi Jaaack. Isn't that moon ride exciting? I've heard it's just the greatest."

"Yeah, it really got the old heart pumping," said Jack. How can she be all smiles, saying what she says and doing what she does? Doesn't anything bother her? Did she just collect bounty money for Howard?

"I bet it did, you poor old thing. Have you been to Dr. Darwin's yet? It's new and very good. You really must take a peek." She fixed Jack in the eye. Jack swallowed.

"Which way?"

"Down this way and to the right," said Susan. "Can't miss it. Want me to come with you?"

"No, I can find it."

"Oookaaay. Have fun!"

Jack walked the way she had pointed and turned right. He had hoped to go directly to the fortune-teller, but now it might look suspicious if he went there immediately. When he joined the crowd at Dr. Darwin's, he noted thankfully that the two were side by side.

A barker dressed in a nineteenth-century suit—complete with top hat, stiff collar and walking stick—held forth on a small platform. Behind him was a door with a dinosaur on each side, forming an arch.

"Yes it is, it is indeed survival of the fittest—that's what I'm saying. It is a jungle out there, my friends, and it's getting worse all the time! Immigration. Automation. Globalization. ANY ONE of these could send you on a long and unpleasant ride on the Down Escalator of our society."

The barker gave the crowd a terrifying look. "Downsizing. Rightsizing. Reengineering. These hit you decades ago—and you still haven't got back on your feet. Am I right? I'm talking major change here! You don't know what's coming at you next, or from which direction. Everything is just OUT OF YOUR CONTROL. You have to be prepared, or you'll end up like one of these!" He smacked a dinosaur with his walking stick.

Two men bearing a stretcher hustled out the door and down into the crowd. The man on the stretcher wore a blue suit with white shirt, red tie and black shoes. He must have fainted.

"Now, what is the best way to avoid that sad gentleman's fate?" the barker continued, gesturing to the departing stretcher. "INFORMATION! Yes! Information. Not brawn, brains. Knowing what's what. Having a clue, ladies and gentlemen! And the best way to do that?" He swept his gaze over the crowd.

"Dr. Darwin's Career Counseling Service!" he bellowed. "Now, I am not Dr. Darwin, no siree. That eminently wise and compassionate gentleman is behind this very door waiting to help you. I am merely trying to give you the vision and the courage to help you help yourself by stepping through this door. You won't regret it, no siree, no."

This was obviously for the badgeless losers who had ponied up their own money. Why had Susan ordered him to come here? He took a deep breath and walked up the steps and through the door.

"Now there's a man not afraid to embrace the future! Do I have any other courageous, productive citizens?"

It was dim inside. Jack climbed up three steps, turned left and walked down a short hallway. A woman, illuminated by spotlights, sat in the center of a room. In front of her was a midget, sitting in a chair placed on a table. His head was too large for his body. A gigantic-seeming can of soda stood next to his chair. A long straw stuck out of the can. He could sip on the straw without picking up the can.

In the shadows behind the midget was a muscleman wearing a leopard-skin leotard. His eyes were gunmetal gray and his face was pitiless. Next to him was a fat lady. At least five hundred pounds. She had a hairy wart on one of her chins. Beside her was a thin man. Around seventy pounds. You could break his arms with your bare hands. The woman in the spotlights stood up.

"Next, please," said the midget.

It was Jack's turn. He sat in the chair and the midget unobtrusively scanned his badge. The muscleman silently closed the curtain behind Jack, then sat at Jack's left.

"I see that your name is Jack?" asked the midget.

"Been jacked around," said the muscleman.

"No longer a crackerjack," said the fat lady.

"Jacked," said the thin man.

"Sure, my name is Jack, but you don't have to be—"

"Jack shit," said the muscleman.

"Jack off," said the fat lady.

"Doesn't know jack," said the thin man.

"Hey, c'mon! I'm a manager. I deserve—"

"Middle management."

"Taking it from above and below."

"Like swimming in a pailful of spit."

"A manager for how long, my dear friend?" asked the midget. "My colleagues are merely helping you clear away old self-conceptions, so that you may see your situation clearly and—"

"Over the hill," said the muscleman.

"Need new blood," said the fat lady.

"Need fresh meat," said the thin man.

"—prepare yourself for the future," concluded the midget.

"It's a new future."

"It's a bright future."

"It's a new and bright future."

Jack wasn't sure how to play this. It might cause problems for him later if he looked too confident now. They were plainly goading him into behavior that would be cause for termination. Failing that, wearing him down and making him want to quit. He decided to be indignant.

"I don't have to take this from you people! I'm a manager, and a good one. I brought my projects in on time and on budget. Before that I was a mechanical engineer, and I was good at that, too. In fact, I have a master's degree in mechanical engineering. I've put in thirty years at the company and I work damn hard. Nights and weekends. Holidays, too. Hardly saw my two kids grow up. This is America. I don't have to listen to this!" He was half out of his chair, shaking his finger at the fat woman and the thin man. He looked at the muscleman. His eyes were steel gray. Jack sat down.

"I assure you I sympathize most thoroughly and with the greatest regard," said the midget. "Nevertheless, I'm afraid one of those weekend projects has rendered you . . . less necessary."

"What are you talking about?"

"Do you recall a Project Helpmate?" replied the midget.

Project Helpmate was that big expert-system project. They had peppered him for months with questions about how he approached his work, how he would solve this or that problem. The goal was to capture his expertise and then produce an intelligent assistant to help the mechanical engineers with their work.

"What about it?" asked Jack.

"It was quite successful. In fact, one could say they captured your expertise rather completely." The midget shrugged his shoulders, as if to suggest that the rest was all too obvious.

Jack's shoulders drooped. He rubbed his forehead and heaved a deep sigh.

"You're history," said the muscleman.

"You're finished," said the fat lady.

"You're toast," said the thin man.

"You're history."

"You're finished."

"You're toast."

"You're history."

"You're finished."

"You're toast."

The chorus stopped and waited for Jack to do something. He looked at the muscleman. The guy was just waiting for an excuse. Jack remembered the liability waiver he had signed on his first trip here. He wondered if anyone had become so enraged that they went berserk. Not Jack. He would rather get even.

"Thank you for your advice. All of you have been very helpful." Jack got up and sauntered out the exit.

Jack rushed next door to the fortuneteller before Susan, or anyone else, could interfere. He parted the curtains and stepped inside. It was dim and smelled of incense.

"Please, come in," said the fortuneteller. "Sit. I will answer all your questions." She had silken robes, big hoop earrings, a phony accent—the works. Her enormous ring contained a laser that scanned his badge.

"Ah, Jack, Jack. Let us look into the crystal ball." The ball was pretty neat. An LCD in the base projected upward into the sphere, creating a globular 3-D effect. The fortuneteller put on a show: waving her hands above the ball, bulging her eyes out, rounding her lips.

"I see . . . I see . . . I see a new life for you. I see you free and happy and untroubled. I see . . ."

"Do you see a pension in my future?" asked Jack. He held his breath. That should trigger it. The fortuneteller made a sour face.

"No! I see—"

She froze. Both of them pressed their noses to the ball.

There was Jack, in bathing trunks, reclining on a deck chair. He was wearing sunglasses and a big smile. A basket was next to him. Every two seconds, an oversized pension check floated through the air and dropped into the basket. Then Jack would pump his right arm and yell out, "Hot damn!"

Jack (the real Jack) loved it. It was a riot. The fortuneteller was aghast. Her carefully rehearsed snow job was just blown away. She frantically mashed the control buttons, but couldn't stop the checks. Finally she gave up and called for help. Jack politely excused himself and walked outside. The chaos spread.

Jack strolled across the midway, climbed the little knoll and took a seat on a bench. This was the best location to watch the uproar. He wanted to enjoy every second of it.

The muzak stopped and good ol' Johnny Paycheck came on, but altered. "You can take this park and shove it—I ain't coming here no more." The badgeless looked perplexed. They had thought they were on the ladder of success. The badged started to grin.

Jack heard screams and looked behind him. A group of retainees was suspended upside down, and far overhead, on the Super Zipper.

No danger. He had checked the safety margins. No matter what the company thought, he was a damn good engineer.

Bells and sirens erupted at the arcade. Every shot at the rifle range was a bull's-eye; every pull on the slots was a jackpot. People screamed and scrambled when the coins gushed out. This was great!

Johnny Paycheck stopped warbling. Another classic screeched out of the loudspeakers, "Don't let the bastards grind you down!" Company employees started laughing and high fiving.

The thin man came running out of Dr. Darwin's, chased by the fat lady. What trick had he played in the confusion? He was running toward the Dark Side of the Moon. If the fat lady caught him and sat on him, that is all he would see. Inside the simulators, the lunar landscape had been replaced by a Pink Floyd concert. Now for the pièce de résistance.

"Will Susan Stanton please report to the cotton-candy machine? Will Susan Stanton please report to the cotton-candy machine?" boomed the loudspeakers.

Susan came running. Jack had put a huge effort into this moment: analyzing the mechanism, tweaking the timings, calculating capacities, tracing trajectories. Still, it was fifty-fifty.

Susan stood there, chaos swirling around her. She turned and the cotton candy machine read her badge. It started blowing a tremendous stream of pink cotton candy at her. She screamed and spun on her heels like a spindle. The sugary candy just kept coming. This was working better than Jack had dared hope. Susan caught a glimpse of him.

"Jack! Jack! Help me! This machine's gone crazy!"

Jack cupped his hands to his mouth. "I think it's a software problem. I'm just an old mechanical engineeeer." He couldn't resist lengthening that last word.

The cotton candy machine ran out of material. Susan stood gasping, surrounded by utter breakdown and pandemonium. Jack tried to fix the scene forever in his memory. It was a six-sigma moment.

Then the program Jack had inserted into the park's software stopped and erased itself. Jack might be a mechanical engineer, but he had seen a few circuit diagrams in his time. Ironically, it was while working on Project Helpmate on the weekends, when security wasn't as tight, that he had vaulted the park's firewall, examined their control software and inserted his voice-activated, self-terminating program.

The park's staff began rushing around, announcing that the park was closing early. The raucous crowd didn't want to hear it at first, but they eventually made for the exits.

Jack took his seat on the bus. His fellow employees were still buzzing excitedly about the breakdown. Two guys were even playing catch with a foam football they had won at the rifle range. Susan was too preoccupied with pulling cotton candy off her clothes to enforce discipline. Howard yelled to someone at the back of the bus.

"Quit? Retire? Naw, I'm having too much fun. I'm too young!" It made Jack smile. He had won for today.

To Jack's engineering way of thinking, it was like a clock's pendulum swinging back and forth: tick, downsizing; tock, insecurity; tick, European-style labor laws; tock, ossification; tick, management mind games; tock, resentment and rebellion. He figured one more tick-tock to go: tick, gross inefficiency from employee sabotage on top of management manipulation on top of fossilization; tock, scrapping the whole rotten edifice and returning, full circle, to downsizing.

That is what he thought. Here is what he felt.

Jack felt happy. He felt human. He felt today was a good day. He even felt he could endure and collect his pension.

The Ascension
of Saint Susan

This is the last rewrite in this collection. I submitted "Her Big Chance" to Ms. Foster's workshop at L.A.con III. The participants gave me many suggestions to improve the story and the quality of the writing. For this version, written in June of 1997, I thought hard about the underlying themes, then tried to make the story more satirical, more ironic and more dramatic.

The Ascension of Saint Susan:
A Thesis/Treatment
(preliminary draft)

Brian Dana Akers
Seminarian/Screenwriter

Dear Rector/Executive Producer:

Here it is—my thesis (footnotes to follow) for my divinity degree, which is also (of course) a treatment for the movie. I want to thank you again for your extraordinarily insightful comments. Any remaining errors of fact and interpretation are entirely my responsibility.

Please note that this is the preliminary draft you wanted to see before I made the final push. I've enclosed my comments in square brackets, [ ], as specified in our seminary's style sheet.

I'm so glad you share my excitement for this project! I have no idea why such a juicy subject wasn't picked up before this. I realize our founders, Jimmy and Kristie, were the main show, but Susan's divinization was just so telegenic! This thesis/treatment is made-for-TV length, but we could expand it in the screenplay stage to feature length. Let's do lunch.

The day I reached up and touched the hem of divinity, becoming divine myself, began with a computer problem.

[As per our previous discussions, though third person with caveats would be more appropriate for a scholarly presentation, this treatment has utilized the first-person POV to facilitate subsequent literary and dramatic presentations.]

Time to call a gook. I hit the tech support button on my phone. Of course, nobody called them "gooks" to their faces, but all of us Lifestyle Specialists called them that when they weren't around. Nothing was really wrong with them, they just weren't with the program. They didn't fit. So polite, so conscientious, so considerate—yuck! [Her generosity and perceptiveness shine through here. She is able to distinguish between the people and their shortcomings.]

I stood up to stretch my legs and look around. My cubicle was in the cavernous CS, the Central Space. Management had lavished a fortune on every surface, just barrels of lacquer. Open walkways suspended from invisible cables crisscrossed above me. Above those, the company logo, PAP, in slender letters on a blue square, glowed down upon us all.

The gook showed up and I tilted my head toward my workstation. He sat in my chair.

"What seems to be the problem?" he asked.

"It's not working right," I replied. I hated this routine. They were the computer experts. Why didn't they just fix it?

"No. I meant, what in particular isn't working right."

"The screen," I said. "The screen isn't working right. Sometimes it gets all wavy and buzzy and I can't read anything on it."

"Okay, give me a minute."

"Yeah, run a test or something."

I pulled out a roll of masking tape and made a loop, sticky side out. Then I checked my clothes, dabbing off pieces of lint. My new suede pocketbook really picked it up. I paused and watched the gook. Black slacks with a white shirt. He looked like a waiter or something. I rolled my eyes and kept dabbing.

Finally, I was totally lint-free. I balled up the tape and threw it away, then shook my thick hair—auburn with chestnut highlights—out over my sweater and gave everything a little jiggle. I popped a piece of gum in my mouth. Everything about me shouted, "I'm a professional!" [Casting will be critical. She has to be just so.]

"I think I see the problem." The gook made a small adjustment and popped the lid back on. "That should do it."

"Great!"

The gook collected his tools and left. Patti, our new Lifestyle intern, passed the gook on his way out. She wrinkled her nose and took an extra half step around him. She caught on quick for a girl who still had some baby fat.

"Computer problems?" asked Patti.

"Yeah," I said. "First the 59th St. Bridge, now this. Not a great day."

Patti came closer and lowered her voice. "I don't even know why we need them, anyway. Doesn't America have enough nerds of its own? I mean, we got universities and stuff, don't we? Somebody must be taking the hard courses. I mean, I didn't, but still."

"You know what really pisses me off about them?" I paused for effect. "Their home countries don't even allow our celebs in!"

"No!" said Patti.

"Yes! Some bullshit about cultural infection and decline. Nonsense about not wanting 'radical individualism.' They want our technology, but not our values."

"Life without our celebs?" She quivered. "Wow."

I offered the kid a seat. "What do you have for me?"

"Some ideas I came up with last night. I don't know if People And Places does this kind of work, but I thought I'd ask you."

"We can leverage almost any idea into something," I replied. "PAP is such a professional organization. Tops. We do research. We do analysis. We do trading for outside accounts. We do trading for in-house accounts. We haven't cracked through to the very highest level—the Bernadettes, the Kristies, the Dianas—but we're almost there. You know the best part about the Research Department, especially here in Lifestyle?"

Breathless, Patti shook her head no.

"We get to focus on the celebs, really get into their lives full-time—and we're getting paid for it!" [Glimmers of Susan's nascent spirituality.]

Patti's face glowed with admiration. [White light, soft filters.]

"Remember all those fan clubs I told you about last week?" I continued. I couldn't resist milking this. "The ones I started when I was a teenager? That was round-the-clock stuff. But it got me noticed as someone to watch. It started me on the path to PAP."

"And you gave all those fans so much to live for. So much, so much . . . meaning," said Patti.

"Meaning," I said.

We fixed each other's gaze.

"Meaning," we said simultaneously.

We paused. It was a meaningful moment.

"So I'll look at your stuff and let you know what I think," I said and stylishly dismissed her. Never hurts to have an ally, no matter how high or how low. [Again, Susan's generosity and compassion.]

I flipped through Patti's ideas. Then my boss, Arni, came running up. His neck was doing that spasm thing again.

"Susan, we have a problem here. Jimmy and Kristie are both in the city and they just held a press conference. They're getting married."

"Married! Jimmy and Kristie!"

"Other firms have started to move on this and the pits in Chicago are sniffing at it. This could break in a big way. PAP needs to know how to position ourselves and our clients. Jimmy and Kristie are holding a public ceremony in Bryant Park late this afternoon. June bride. The whole nine yards."

"Bryant Park? Behind the 42nd Street Library? Man, they're really sticking it to them. This is serious."

"I know," said Arni, twitching. "It's risky. You're our Kristie person. Start putting together your POV." He hurried off.

I called up the press conference on my workstation.

There they were, Jimmy and Kristie proclaiming that they loved each other and were getting married. The interviewer was skeptical and kept asking Kristie what she saw in Jimmy. Kristie, sparkling and shimmering, merely smiled that billion-dollar smile. This was obviously Jimmy's chance to move up and get some class. He just sat there with a big grin on his face. [This is clearly a delicate scene. My research unequivocally shows that Susan was skeptical at first. If one is to be a true scholar, one has to remember that the world—and the way people looked at it—was different back then. The historical polling data indicates that the most common initial reaction to the marriage was in fact skepticism. A good actress can convey these nuances just by raising an eyebrow.]

I played it through a second time, then a third. No lunch for me today. I didn't know what to think. Kristie sounded like she loved the guy. But I had followed Kristie my whole life. This wasn't a Kristie thing to do.

Ted might have an angle on this. I walked through the CS to Trading. I opened the massive glass door and stepped inside.

No matter how much they filtered the air in here, you could always smell the sweat. Today looked like a one-and-a-half-phone day: Some traders had one phone to their heads, some had two. You could still hear yourself think, if you thought loud enough. With this marriage, it could develop into a full three-phone day.

The Jimmy and Kristie interview was cycling through on the big screen. Sober and dignified commentators were dispensing solemn judgments on the banks of smaller screens. One screen showed swarms of reporters massing outside Kristie's building, demanding a follow-up statement. Trading's staff was hustling to stay on top of the situation. I dodged my way to Ted's station and sat beside him.

"How's the action?" I asked.

He pulled his eyes away from his screen. "Hey Susan. The Kristie thing? The pits in Chicago have decided to go with it. So far it's just simple futures and options and nothing too exotic. It hasn't overflowed into stocks yet. The Dow is off ninety, but that could be due to other things. The benchmark Bowie bonds are unchanged—probably waiting for direction from stocks."

I absorbed the information. "Remember that time we went to lunch? You were telling me something like all the information in the universe was built into the market? That it was a consensus of all the best brains?" [This might be a good place for a special effects dream sequence to expand on that old saw about doing good by doing well. Calvin somebody, I think. The magic of the market . . . all those people staring intently at their screens . . . Saint Michael's "greed is good" ethos and so on.]

Ted nodded.

"So what are all the best brains saying?"

"They're saying they don't know yet," replied Ted.

"No trend?" The trend is your friend. I remembered that clearly from our lunch.

"No trend."

I smiled. "Thanks, Ted. You've been a big help." I didn't say anything about another lunch in the future. I stood up and walked out of Trading. I could feel his eyes on my hips. [Holy charisma.]

The sweet smell of hair gel saturated the air in the CS. I sat back down at my workstation and pulled up my files on Jimmy and Kristie. Time was running out and I still didn't have a feel for the marriage. My stomach growled. I pored over my files for more than an hour. Arni came by, hovered, twitched and left without saying a word.

Analysis might have a handle on this by now. I got up and walked through the CS again, past the chaos in Trading and down the long corridor to what Lifestyle had nicknamed the Silent Tomb of Analysis.

I quietly opened the door and asked the gatekeeper, "Who is handling the Jimmy and Kristie marriage?"

"Margaret."

I froze, then swallowed.

"I'll let her know you're coming," said the gatekeeper cheerfully, pushing a button on her console. I took a deep breath and walked down to Margaret's office. Ruffled quants looked up from their screens as I passed each of their cubicles. I tapped on Margaret's door. She opened it.

"Susan. Come in. Sit down. Maybe you'll learn something," said Margaret, sniffing. I closed the door behind me and took a seat.

Oh oh. Bad-eyes day. When Margaret's contacts bothered her, her eyes became bloodshot. Then she would switch to her large thick glasses. However, Margaret didn't like the way she looked in glasses and was therefore more disagreeable than usual. Her frumpy dress didn't do much for her either. [It was so beautiful when my research proved what I thought must be true was true—Margaret was ugly! It was an epiphany for me. Her ugliness/cynicism is a perfect symbolic counterpoint to Susan's beauty/belief.]

Margaret started in. "Let's look at the implications of the marriage to see if it makes any business sense. On one side you have Jimmy, who has clawed his way out of the house music scene to cobble together a whole house-grunge-street music combine. [Our

Lord's humble beginnings.] Extensive network of thugs to protect his distribution. Possibly involved in several homicides himself, but never charged. [An authentic voice of the downtrodden.] Executive ability and ambition. Tough. Main problem is cracking the mainstream broadcasting and distribution networks, to say nothing of anemic international penetration. Receives only disrespect on news and opinion shows. Good connections with some politicians. Sports connections are best in boxing. Getting a foothold in the action picture end of Hollywood. Probably his greatest strength is in music videos.

"Now let's look at Kristie. The major talent at a classy pop combine, but unlike Jimmy, doesn't run her own show. Totally legit and above board, by all appearances. Has spent heavily to create and maintain those appearances. Excellent domestic distribution and one of the few celebs—as you no doubt call them—who has penetrated foreign markets. That's how squeaky clean she is. [Focus groups say a virgin-birth type of angle won't fly in the early twenty-first century no matter how saturated the campaign. Rats.] Gets interviewed frequently and fawningly in the mainstream media. Sang at one inauguration. Starred in a string of movies. Her main problem is that she doesn't run her own show. Also aging demographics. Also high favorables, but not intensely held favorables."

Margaret just loved to lecture. [Lecturing is a problem for us, as I learned on day one of my parables/plotting class. I'm leaving this exposition in for this thesis/treatment. We'll take most of it out for the general release. It may work as an optional insert for a young adult educational version, but we would have to convert it to eye candy to hold their attention.]

"So who is behind this and why?" asked Margaret. "We've been modeling since the announcement, but it's still impossible to say who is serving what interests. Certainly the existing combines and syndicates don't want a major new independent entity. That's been accurately conveyed by the tone of their station's commentaries—negative, but not so negative as to risk losing their slice of Kristie's action. Curiously, Kristie's own combine is essentially silent, merely issuing a brief statement saying that marriage is a matter of the heart. Hah! Who would fall for that one?" Margaret paused and looked directly at me.

You bitch, I thought, and smiled sweetly. [Again, a good actress can convey this devastatingly with just a look.]

Margaret continued. "If I may digress a moment, we're very excited about our current research on the increasingly keiretsu nature of the American economy. Beyond keiretsu, in fact. Just incredible cross-industry linkages everywhere. Almost like the hair-trigger situation described so well in *The Guns of August*. A heap of delicately piled swords. You do know what a keiretsu is and you have read *The Guns of August*, haven't you? Oh, I forgot who I was talking to." Margaret threw herself back in her chair and rolled her eyes at the ceiling.

I had had enough. I didn't like the way everyone in PAP outside the Research department talked about celebs. They just didn't know what celebs meant to people! [This is faith! This is integrity! This is what makes us great!]

"Okay, so—what does this marriage mean?"

Margaret blinked. "Well, you tell me. You're the expert on Kristie. What do you think?"

"I'm . . . I'm not sure."

Margaret stared at me for a moment, then continued. "What's driving this relationship—besides money and status, of course? As I was saying, cross-industry linkages. It might be Hollywood and not music at all. If it is Hollywood, then politics is definitely involved."

Margaret cocked her head to one side. "A marriage to Jimmy would allow foreign governments to withdraw access rights for Kristie without risking sanctions from our government. Hmm. Asia certainly has had an influential role in world affairs ever since our own culture and economy became celebrity driven. Hmm. If politics is involved, any realignment could be swift and shattering. This could be what moves 'us,'" she shuddered, "to the front of the trough."

Margaret mulled it over. "Well, there you have my thoughts on the matter. Our simulations have been inconclusive. Trading still reports no . . ."

Margaret's workstation started screeching. She looked at the screen. "Oh my god! Everything's moving!" [This should be one of those classic "scramble" scenes that the old Holy Land did so well. You know, where everyone leaps into action, the strings are playing 32nd notes, etc.]

I took off without saying goodbye—or thanks. I looked over my shoulder into Trading as I ran past. It was a hockey brawl in there.

Everybody in the CS had abandoned their cubicles and mobbed the windows. I elbowed my way in and looked down. It took my breath away.

Madison Avenue was paved with gold.

Wow. This was so Zen.

[Soundtrack goes to dead silence—the sound of one hand writing campaign slogans.]

The staff babbled. "Awesome special effect!" "It was normal just five minutes ago." "How did they do it?" "It's our turn now!" I caught Arni's eye and yelled out, "I'm going to Bryant Park!" Then I skipped the elevator and took off down the stairs before he could say no.

Thank God for high heels, sharp elbows and an attitude. [Her zeal to merge with the Godhead.] Party animals jammed the stair-well and Mardi Gras filled the air. I joined the throng surging down the yellow brick road to Bryant Park.

Kristie's people had closed off two blocks of Sixth Avenue and set up a superbowl-class stage. The buzz of the crowd was building.

I elbowed my way through. Every time I reached another security perimeter, I flashed my PAP badge. It was like the word of God to them. Only the final line of security wouldn't let me through unless I really was God.

Present at the creation, I kept telling myself, present at the creation. The electricity of the Garden, but more intense. And it wasn't the Knicks; it was history. I could see the yearning in their faces as they bounced on their toes.

The bass line throbbed louder. Smoke, light and lasers. Jimmy and Kristie materialized. The crowd thundered. It was always a thrill to see a big celeb in person, but to see these two on this occasion—awesome.

Kristie was a diaphanous vision of feminine splendor unmatched in history. Her signature Kristie's Ultimate Jasmine™ perfume wafted into the audience. She stood at the front of the stage on the left. Jimmy strode back and forth behind her, getting pumped up for the crowd and the cameras. He started in his rap-preacher style.

"Ladies and gentlemen, we are gathered here to-day to join myself and this woman in ho-ly ma-tri-mo-ny." When he said "this woman," Kristie struck a pose and the crowd cheered. Nobody struck a pose better than Kristie. The gaffers had come up with a new technique that put a subtle shimmering aura around her.

"Ladies and gentlemen, we are gathered here to-day to usher in a new age. An age with a new church, a new holy city, new values, and a new first couple. Mm mm mm." Kristie struck a pose. The crowd screamed in rapture. [This is what sends chills down my spine: The founders of our church were captured on film. They aren't lost in the distant past like Jesus, Buddha and all those other guys.]

"Just like the streets up in heaven are paved with gold, so too is Madison Avenue, the birthplace of American genius. It is the new Via Dolorosa. It is our very own road to the stars." The crowd was his. [How could they not have been? This is a brilliant thematic statement, a dense assemblage of high-impact keywords.]

"Where are all the stars? Where is that golden road leading us to? To Hollywood. To Hollywood! Some of those big-ass letters up in the hills are coming down—coming down! Some new letters are going up—going up! And the sign is gonna say 'Holy Land.'" Kristie placed her palms together and bowed her head. It was way too late to quiet this crowd.

"The motion-picture academy will be our new church. The academy awards will be bigger that Christmas, biggerrrr than Christ-mas.

"We're gonna have some new values, some new values. Values that are pretty, values that don't make you feel bad, values that you can take pride in, values that take pride in you, values of excellence— PRODUCTION VALUES!" Then Jimmy grabbed his crotch and thrust it toward the library. Boom! Two library windows shattered. They were really sticking it to the bookworms. Sticking it!

"Listen up, y'all. If you produce that cigarette package just right, you have created a thing of beauty. Take pride in your technique. You ain't done nothin' wrong! Who can really tell right from wrong?

"But everyone can tell when something is done well.

"In our new church, I'll make you the Pope of Packaging! The Pontiff of Picas and Points! The Prince of Product Placement!"

I was a little dizzy at this point. It was our turn now. Us. And I was present at the creation. Yet even in the middle of this, I could see problems. The Writers Guild wasn't going to like accepting their awards late, so FX could hog prime time. Editors of those dreadfully produced little science fiction magazines would no doubt blather on about "story, story, story." Pompous cranks from Ann Arbor, Oberlin and places like that would produce reams of very dull copy. All the old religions wouldn't consider us a religion at all.

Screw them. [Righteous indignation.] It would be a rear-guard action. There hadn't been an original movie in decades; Hollywood just kept remaking the old ones with better production values. Production values already were the values of our society.

[The dramatic irony here is delicious: The formation of our church created a whole new source of stories. Stories we can tell with proper production values right from the start.

Still, they have to be pitched just right for the good of our church. The founder of our order was very wise to start this seminary/screenwriting school immediately. Our points on the gross are building a handsome endowment for future generations of scholars.]

I snapped back to the present. Jimmy strutted over and put his arm around Kristie. "That new first couple? Ain't we fine?" A dozen women fainted then and there.

"We're bigger than the Beatles! And you know who they were bigger than." I looked behind me and saw a geezer fumble in his pocket for a roach at the mention of the Beatles.

"Now let us form a procession up our new golden avenue." Two thrones rose out of the stage. The stage reassembled itself into a giant float. It slowly moved right in front of me. Kristie's gown blew toward me. I quickly stepped around a guard to touch it. It made ermine feel like sandpaper. Then Kristie looked down at me—at me—and waved me to a seat on the float. I climbed up and sat in a daze. The multitude of cameras beamed it around the world as we progressed up Madison Avenue.

They were divinity, and I was the first acolyte, the first apostle. [BIG FINISH!!!]

Needless to say, that was really good for my career. I shot up through the PAP org chart, dragging Patti along behind me to cover my ass. It's amazing the way a great-looking sweater can open doors for you. [Preordained and foreshadowed.]

I think we're going to have quite a run, too. Really change society, make everything slick and shiny. It's funny how, for most people, knowing all the ins and outs, the behind-the-scenes details, doesn't seem to matter. I think all the talk shows over the decades conditioned them. The gossip just makes our church all the more compelling. [This was puzzling to me as a novice seminarian/screenwriter. It was only after I took the core courses on Candor that I realized how tricky and delicate this is.]

One thing though: We can't stand having the gooks around. They don't follow fashion, they don't style their hair, and those big computer manuals they carry around are just horribly produced. So we're going to use our clout and have them all deported. Just send them back to Taiwan, Korea, India—wherever the hell they came from, we'll send them back.

I mentioned this to some guy from Madison (I should've known better) over lunch one day. He actually had the nerve to come back at me with that old sitcom line, "Pride goeth before a fall." Then he added some gobbledygook about "Production values are the marriage of vapidity and technology. Without the foreigners, things will simply stop working."

What a jerk that guy was. I looked him straight in the eye and said, "Pick up the clue phone. We're number one." [A look of withering superiority. Casting! Casting!]

[Denouements are always tricky. Remember the film version of 2010? As you know, our relationship with the international labor market is ongoing and complex. We will have to revise the ending at the last minute to promote our upcoming diplomatic initiatives. I've heard these initiatives will involve building bridges to celebrities overseas. They're our natural allies in making people everywhere more like us.

The problem really comes down to this: How do we maintain access to foreign expertise without contaminating our culture?]

May/December
at the Mall

The coolest thing about this story? I was personally invited by Jim Baen to contribute to the Chicks 'n Chained Males *anthology. Presold! No sending it out to magazine after magazine! After the initial elation and wonderment subsided, panic set it in. What if I couldn't deliver?*

I had been thinking that my stories were too much about ideas and setting, and not enough about characters and plot, so I focused on the characters when I wrote this in May of 1998.

The anthology had just three requirements: a women rescuing men theme, be humorous, and feature women and armor in combination. So check, check and check. Enjoy.

Katya crouched under a palm tree in the food court of the Mall of Alternate Americas. She had picked a two seater with an excellent field of view. Her triple cheeseburger was history; just a few fries left. It was lunchtime and the court was filling up. Someone would be asking for the other seat soon. She merely had to pick the right wildebeest.

A teenage boy with a hopeful smile wearing a leather jerkin approached. Katya glared at him and dropped her hand to her hilt. He wisely pivoted ninety degrees. A fat abbess got the same treatment. Then Katya saw a tall, thin, older man—not an old man, just suitably older than Katya—holding his little orange tray and looking for a seat. She gave him a big smile and motioned him over.

"Have a seat," said Katya.

"Thanks." The man sat down. He had a veggie burger, salad, and some kind of fruit drink.

"Wow," said Katya. "Veggie burger and salad. You really live on the edge." She crinkled her nose.

He gave a little shrug. "There are old travelers, and there are bold travelers, but there are no old, bold travelers."

"A traveler? You're sure you're not an accountant?" asked Katya.

"I'm a survivor. Only the prudent survive."

"Oh, let's all be prudent. That sounds like lots of fun!"

He frowned and bit into his burger. Travelers from every era were filling the court: knights in self-shining armor, damsels distressed by impossibly thick sandwiches, samurai discussing hara-kiri techniques, and Aztecs preparing to sacrifice combination platters to their own personal stomach gods.

Katya slowly bit another fry. She tried not to be too obvious. "I'm sorry. Here I am teasing you and we haven't even introduced ourselves. My name is Katya."

"Reimann."

"Where are you from, Reimann?" She batted her eyelashes.

"Just got back from seventeenth-century China. Picked up some incredible silks. A few paintings. Statuary. Vases."

"Are you a merchant?" Katya could practically see the words "sugar daddy" tattooed on his forehead.

"I'm a . . . conservator," said Reimann. His shoulders sagged. "Some time streams get the hell pillaged out of them. They're not healthy. I'm trying to save some of it." He stared at his burger. "I'm just one person."

She paused to process that. "You're very dedicated."

"Mm," said Reimann. He glanced at her and forked his salad.

"No, really. A lot of people wouldn't shoulder that burden. They would just go with the flow. People like me." She winked and laughed.

"It's hopeless. I just feel way out of it. Too much looping through time. I'm out of phase and time-lagged." Reimann frowned and stabbed his salad again. His eyes got that thousand-year stare.

Katya looked down and concentrated on her fries. This was a bad turn. She had dealt with guys in futures shock before. They became so distant and detached that they weren't good for anything. She would have to snap him out of it, quick.

"You know a great time to kick ass? The late Roman Empire. Tops. They're all a little slow from the lead poisoning." She pulled her short Roman sword out of its scabbard and clanged it down so hard on the table that Reimann jumped in his seat. The food court went dead silent for a moment as everyone assessed the risk of a fight. Katya's face flushed. She fixed Reimann in the eye.

"You old guys keep thinking it's going back to the way it was. It's not. Loosen up. Have some fun."

Reimann focused on her and gave a dry laugh. "Girls just want to have fun."

"Now those are words to live by!" said Katya. "Want to hear a few more? Let's go shopping!"

Reimann laughed louder. "Okay, kiddo, whaddiya say we go and buy you some new chain mail?"

Katya's eyes sparkled. "Kiddo? Kiddo? You're calling me kiddo? You're not that much older than me. At least, I think you're not."

Katya popped the last fry in her mouth. Both stood up, dumped their trays and stacked them on top of the trashcan. She grabbed his hand and squeezed it playfully.

"Just follow me. You're not married, are you?"

"No, I'm young and virile and on the prowl." Reimann laughed again. Katya laughed too. It was such a cute thing for prey to say. "And you're a blonde with brains, boobs, baby fat, and ebullience. Just my type."

Katya laughed. This was more like it.

"Which store?" asked Reimann.

"Definitely Cleopatra's Closet. Definitely." Katya waited for him to object. Either he didn't know the store, or he had money.

They strolled through the mall, getting to know each other. The kiosks that used to sell flight insurance now sold temporal insurance. Reimann growled that it was a scam—time-line arbitrage that was helping screw everything up. When they passed a T-shirt store, Katya had to stop and read each shirt.

"Hey, this one's for you: Old age and treachery will triumph over youth and inexperience."

"I'm not treacherous. I'm sweet." He grinned.

She smiled and held his hand. "This is great. 'When the going gets tough, the tough go shopping.' That's my philosophy."

Reimann laughed. "You and everyone else. That's why this place is a neutral zone."

"Neutral zone?" asked Katya.

"For R and R. For shore leave," said Reimann. "Agora . . . bazaar . . . market . . . mall. There's always some place like this in every time stream. Always some place to shop."

Katya had never heard it put quite that way before. The muzak just made the mall seem so ordinary. "Do you understand how it all happened?" she asked. "Every explanation I've heard sounded like a lot of arm waving to me."

Reimann looked thoughtful. "Not really. What's the first cause of anything? Somehow temporal streamers weakened the tensegrity of our old unitary space-time and frayed it into all these strands." Katya let him talk. Maybe talking would help him get it out of his system.

"Sometimes I can almost feel immense loops of time coming into the mall, like the ribbons of Earth's magnetic field. For these few decades, Minnesota is important. For other times, other places.

"Oh, you know, speaking of other places, someone from the twenty-fourth was telling me Da Lat is a cool little town."

"Never heard of it. Where is it?" asked Katya.

"Vietnam. Central Highlands. During the American phase of the war, all parties had a tacit agreement to spare the town. In fact, officials from both sides, from time to time and without knowing it, rented villas side by side. I want to check it out sometime. Come with me?"

"Da Lat. Right. I'm sure." She rolled her eyes.

"Hey, here we are. Cleopatra's Closet. Isn't it cool?" said Katya. They admired the window displays.

"Very authentic looking," said Reimann. "Hell, it probably is authentic."

"The real thing? Great! Let's go!"

The store wasn't exactly Egyptian—more like the boudoir of a Moorish princess. Clothes were tucked away in a fantastic collection of armoires and chests. Browsing there was like rummaging through her private affairs. The atmospherics simulated a late afternoon in Spain. It was elegantly done.

A saleswoman sized up the situation instantly. "Welcome to our store. My name is Serafina. What would the young lady be looking for today?" She lowered her voice. "When not in Rome, don't do as the Romans do. You need new chain mail."

"Don't I know it!" said Katya. "Which way to the heavy-duty battle stuff? I want a complete suit." Serafina was thrilled to oblige.

Katya squealed when she opened the giant armoire. "They have everything here! Everything!"

"I can put together some very attractively priced ensembles for you, too," said Serafina. "We have all the major patterns—birdcage, oriental six-on-one, Persian three-on-one—and most of the minor ones as well. It's all done in the latest synthetics. Strong and very light." Reimann sighed and sank into an overstuffed leather armchair.

Katya darted into the dressing nook with a chain-mail brassiere. The cups were a little small, making her look quite ample. She tucked and jiggled and bounced and wiggled. She threw her hair back. Time to give Reimann a quiz.

She stepped out and asked (in all apparent innocence), "Do I look fat in this?"

Reimann fixed her in the eye and said, "Absolutely not. That one looks great on you. If anything, you're too thin. You're ravishing. You're stunning."

"Oh, you're so sweet, Reimann."

She kept turning around in front of the mirror, undecided.

"I think, though," added Reimann, "that if you're going back to, oh, the eleventh or twelfth, you'll want more protection."

Katya left the brassiere on and started hefting the swords.

"That rapier," said Serafina, "has a matching dagger with a hidden cavity for poisons. It's an exquisite set. I'm sure I can do something on the price. Trade-in for your Roman stuff, something."

"I think the rapier clashes with the brassiere," said Reimann. "They're from completely different eras and countries."

Serafina leaned over and whispered in Katya's ear. "Purists. Can't stand them. We'll send him away in a few moments. Make sure he leaves his credit card." She straightened up and told Reimann, "Excellent observation. I recommend we begin with the body armor and accessorize afterwards."

Katya went nuts trying on different pieces of armor. Reimann cautioned her about helmets that were too bulky or poorly ventilated, warned her how finicky the joints could be in French armor, and generally tried to speed the decision-making process. Katya beamed when she had, at last, selected an ensemble.

"Some people say money can't buy happiness. I say they just don't know where to shop."

"Jesus, you're deep," said Reimann.

Serafina looked thrilled. "I have some wonderful lingerie that would set off that armor quite nicely. You know, for after the battle. One mustn't forget that you're a woman, as well as a warrior."

"Oh God," moaned Reimann. He looked at his watch and sagged deeper into his chair. He looked like a broken man.

"Oh, you poor thing," said Katya. "You don't have to sit though this, too. Just leave me your card, and I'll come find you afterwards."

Reimann reached into his wallet and handed her one of his credit cards. "Really? Can I go? Really? You won't mind?"

Katya plucked the card away. "Of course not. Why should you have to suffer?"

Reimann's sudden reprieve seemed to give him a burst of energy. He gathered his limbs and made a beeline out of the store. Katya flourished his card and grinned.

"Let the games begin!" she cried.

After Katya was accoutered, accessorized, auxiliarized, generally armed to the teeth (and such good friends with Serafina), she left the store to look for Reimann. She strolled past Missile Gap, Missile Gap Kids, and Baby Missile Gap. She peeked into Krazy Katapults, searched Dragons for a Dollar, and scoped out Onagers R Us.

She was starting to worry when she heard girls' voices coming from a men's room. That ain't right, she thought. Katya looked up and down the hall, but didn't see anyone who looked like mall security. She checked that her armor was secure, gripped her shield and drew her rapier.

Then she kicked the door in.

There was Reimann, chained spreadeagled to a bathroom stall. His mouth was gagged and his feet dangled above the floor. Five teenage girls, smoking cigarettes and wearing heavy makeup, looked toward the door.

"Be gone, you little mall rats!" cried Katya.

She weighed into the gang of girls, splitting them into two groups—two to her right, three to her left. She spun to her right and grazed the first girl with the tip of her rapier. The girl backed to the wall and started sidestepping to the door.

"Where are you going?" screamed the second girl. She turned her head toward the first and Katya butted her with her shield. Girl number two crawled for the door.

Katya instantly wheeled to face the remaining three. She crab-stepped toward Reimann, so they couldn't harm him or hold him hostage. The ringleader tried to look tough by swinging her chain. Katya looked down.

"I think you'll find oversized jeans a liability in combat—besides looking incredibly stupid."

When the ringleader glanced down at her baggy jeans, Katya caught her chain with the tip of her rapier and flung it aside. The ringleader lunged for it. Katya smacked her in the ass with the flat of her blade and sent her flying. The remaining two girls broke and ran after their friends.

"And smoking is prohibited in all restrooms!" Katya yelled after them.

Katya turned to Reimann. Her face was flushed with the excitement of battle. Sweat trickled down her forehead. Her breasts heaved. She grinned with relief and ungagged him.

"Reimann, what happened?"

"Mall chicks in chains."

He gasped for breath. "I was lost in thought when I walked in here. Then I heard the door latch behind me and looked up and there they were. I knew I was in trouble. I said, 'You can't do this. This is neutral territory.' And they said, 'We ain't time travelers, jerk. We're locals.' Then they gagged me and chained me up and debated the pros and cons of various indignities. I couldn't believe I had stumbled into this mess. I didn't know what I was going to do. Then you burst in the door like an avenging angel. God, you were magnificent!"

Katya loosened the chains and lowered Reimann to the floor. She wet a paper towel and wiped his face.

"I have you to thank for the armor, you know."

"Money well spent." He smiled.

"You know what you were saying about the time streams not being as healthy as they should be? I shouldn't have laughed at you. You were right. This shouldn't have happened."

Katya looked into his eyes. They lost their thousand-year stare and gazed back into her eyes. The eons, the centuries, the hours evaporated away until only this moment existed, and Reimann was in it and no other.

"I . . . I feel young again."

Katya couldn't fight back a small sob. She gave him a close hug and then snapped her head back.

"You do!"

Continuing Ed

I heard Michael Fossel speak, then read his book, Reversing Human Aging, *which provided most of the scientific basis for this story I wrote in December of 1998, along with then-current reports on stem cells and gene therapy. Pretty cool stuff. But what do we do with eternally young retirees?*

Becky Simmons checked over her lesson plans. A framed photograph of last year's graduation ceremony anchored the left corner of her desk. It was the proudest moment of her life. She felt she made a difference every day—although some days were better than others. Some classes were better than others, too. In fact, this class was the slowest one yet. Becky could hear them yelling in the hall.

"Apple. I bought Apple. Love it. It's gonna split. I love stocks that split. Then you own twice as much." That would have to be Louise, allocating society's capital in the most efficient way possible.

"Bonds," replied Bob. "Can't go wrong with government bonds. You can sleep at night, too, that's for sure."

The bell rang. They trooped in and took their seats. Becky stood up and faced the class. Every one of them had such smooth, lustrous skin. Teeth were a bit iffy, though.

"Thank you for your attention," said Becky. "As you know, today is our final class together and—" The class broke into applause. She hated when classes did that. "—And we're going to spend the period reviewing the three main points; the three main reasons why you're all here. Now, who can tell me the first reason?" Bob jumped halfway up and thrashed his arm. "Okay, Bob, what's the number one reason we're here today?"

"Tell-o-meters! Tell-o-meters!" said Bob. Louise snickered.

"Very close," replied Becky. "However, the correct word is telomere. Telomere."

"But I remember it as tell-o-meter. That's my knee-monic device. 'Cause it's like a meter telling you how old you are!" Bob beamed triumphantly.

Becky took a deep breath. "Very good. Now, can anyone tell me what a telomere is?" Georgette raised her hand. "Georgette?"

"It's the doohickey at the end of the thingamajig." Everybody started to laugh.

"Chromosome," yelled Becky. "Not thingamajig, chromosome!"

"Wanna hear my knee-monic for chromosome?" asked Bob.

"No, I do not want to hear your mnemonic for chromosome!" This crowd was giving Becky gray hair. She pushed on. "Can anyone tell me the difference between telomerase inhibition and telomerase inducement?"

Amos stood up and cleared his throat. "That one I can most definitely answer, having beaten the big C myself." The class gave him a round of applause. Amos stood tall and continued. "Inhibitors shorten telomeres and are used to treat cancer. Inducers lengthen telomeres and are used to prevent and reverse aging. It's those inducers that make us such a fine-looking bunch." He sat down.

"Oy vey, those inducers," said Louise. "I never should've bothered with this face lift." She pulled out her yarn and began knitting.

"I know I feel younger," said Harold. "And that whole Viagra routine is history." He reached forward and pinched Georgette on the butt. She squealed. Then she turned around and batted her eyelashes—twice.

"All right, all right!" Becky grabbed her marble nameplate and smashed it down on her desk. "Enough already! The second reason. Can anyone tell me the second reason you're still here?"

Lorne raised his hand. He was a retired sheriff. Becky nodded at him. "Go ahead, Lorne." He cleared his throat.

"I have made a considerable, in-depth study of this topic and I must report, although I am in no ways an expert, that the most important factor contributing to a long life is getting those free radicals off the streets—the streets here being a metaphor for your blood vessels and such, you understand."

"Simile," said Georgette.

"No, I said metaphor, and I meant metaphor."

"Simile."

"Metaphor." He folded his arms across his chest.

Becky exploded. "Metaphor, simile, analogy—whatever! It's wrong. The second thing is—can anyone tell me the second thing?" Bob raised his hand again. "Okay, Bob. Tell us."

"Stencils."

"Stencils?"

"Stencils."

Becky froze. What on earth was he talking about?

"I think he means stem cells," said Louise. "It isn't very good, his English." She sniffed.

Becky sat and put her face in her hands. "Yes. Stem cells. Stem cells. Not stencils. Stem cells. Can anyone tell me the role stem cells play in longevity?" Harold raised his hand. "Okay, Harold, what do they do?"

"It's fixup work, basically. Stem cells give us the repair material; sort of like a piece of lumber. You want to make it part of a desk, it's part of a desk. You want to make it part of a chair, it's part of a chair. Handy stuff."

Lorne stood up. "I would just like to take this opportunity to say a few words about exactly where these stem cells originate, and whether or not we should be harvesting these itty bitty——"

Becky interrupted. "We talked about that in our third session. That question was settled back in 2005. We're not going into it again."

"It may be settled as far as you're concerned, but——"

"Yes, it is settled as far as the Supreme Court and today's class is concerned. That will do it for stem cells. Keep your booklet. It has lots of technical information that you can refer to in the future." Becky looked at her watch. "Okay. So, we've talked about telomere therapy, and we've talked briefly about stem cells. What is the third major reason you're all here today?"

This time Corey raised his hand. Everyone groaned. Corey was the slowest person in the class.

"Yes, Corey, what is the third reason?"

"Jean therapy."

Becky blinked. She couldn't believe he knew the answer. "Very good, Corey! That's right, gene therapy. Gene therapy is the third big thing. Can you tell us more about how gene therapy is done?"

"Oh, uh, there are many different kinds, you know, kinds, all kinds of kinds, done different ways, all kinds of ways. Some kinds are more popular than other kinds—the less popular kinds." He shut up.

Becky wasn't sure whether she should follow up with Corey, or ask someone else. She looked at Corey. "Yes, many different techniques have been invented, developed, introduced and modified over the past twenty years. Name the most popular."

Corey had the most intense deer-in-the-headlights look she had ever seen. Then he blurted it out. "Stone washing."

The whole class burst out laughing. Something died inside Becky right then. She just hoped whatever it was could be rejuvenated.

"Okay, this is how it is," said Becky. "Starting out, you're a mess. You're old, you're broken down, you're full of time bombs waiting to go off. Telomere therapy makes you young again—or at least keeps you from getting older. Therapies derived from stem cells repair what's already broken. That leaves the time bombs. Even with the first two, you still have bad genes here and there between your telomeres. And if you're living longer, they have more chances to cause you problems. So the third part is gene therapy."

Becky looked at her watch. She had one minute left. "Look. It's 2020. The world is changing faster and faster; progress is happening every day. How are you—you *goofballs*—going to keep up? Your bodies are young, but your minds are still old. You need to think young, too. How are you even going to earn a living?'"

It was silent for a moment.

"Send us a check," said Harold.

All of them, every one of them, guffawed like geezers—slapping their thighs, snorting like pigs, cackling like hens. Their body language was straight out of the mid-twentieth century.

"Thank you so much for teaching this class," said Louise. "I like to see the young people of today gainfully employed. You know—paying FICA." They hooted and hollered at that one, too.

"Send us a check," Harold said again. That kept the laughs rolling.

"Class dismissed," said Becky. The boisterous gang of soft-skinned geezers bolted from the room.

Becky looked at her graduation picture and shook her head. They really did mean "send us a check." The Social Security Administration had tried to changeover to electronic transfer payments twenty years ago, but a small group of determined seniors would have none of it. They had money, they had time, they were organized—and those who wanted them kept receiving paper checks.

Becky felt dizzy. She put her head down on her desk. The world was spinning faster and faster—and slower and slower—at the same time.

Falling Forward

We'll conclude this collection with a nonfiction essay. Originally subtitled, "A Science Fiction Writer Looks at the Twenty-First Century," this was my contribution to millennial prognostication. I wrote it in November of 1999. So far, it has proven to be a very solid piece of work.

It was published in Chronogram, *a regional arts monthly, and also extracted for a lesson in* Focus on IELTS. *The primary source of statistics was the Worldwatch Institute's* Vital Signs *series.*

I hope you enjoyed this collection of my early work. I took a pause in my fiction writing to translate and publish some of the classic Yoga texts in Sanskrit-English editions. That effort will continue, but I will also write more stories when the muse drops by.

Contrary to popular belief, science fiction writers usually don't make predictions—especially about the future. They claim they are not in the prediction business, that they are just laying the possibilities on the table, giving the reader a chance to walk around and sniff the air in a variety of possible futures. Mostly, though, they just don't want to look like fools.

Although science fiction has had its moments of prescience—atomic energy and space travel come to mind—it has also suffered from myopia. Think about it. Have you ever seen flying cars, personal helicopters, or jet packs in the Galleria parking lot? Have you bought your summer togas yet? Come to think of it, shouldn't we be wearing all-white by now instead of all-black? More seriously, do you realize that science fiction gave us plenty of giant, electronic brains—but did not foreshadow personal computers? It's true. What's more, you'd be hard-pressed to find a science fiction novel in which the USSR simply . . . dissolved.

I honestly don't know why everyone else is so bad at foreseeing the future. It's not so tough. Here is the straight skinny on the next century. In fact, clip this article and check in with me in 2100. We'll go over the list together—we both might still be around.

I've divided my predictions into four categories: Written in Stone, Slam Dunks, Probable, and Possible. The alert reader will notice that I don't always specify quantities. (Will sea level rise by two centimeters, or two meters? Will the number of species decrease by hundreds, or hundreds of thousands? No one knows.) Note, also, that I'm looking at the entire world, not just the United States. Finally, although it's often said that we are living in the post-modern world, I disagree. With half the people in the world yet to make their first phone call, we are only halfway through the modern era that began two centuries ago.

Written in Stone

You can absolutely count on the following happening.

• Massive, rapid change. The twenty-first century will be the make-or-break century for Planet Earth. Immense transformations of all kinds—political, social, economic, and more—will rumble through the century, driven primarily by the twin forces of demography (which has incredible mass) and technology (which has incredible velocity). Our green valley will not escape the whirlwind. Lift your gaze up from that copy of *Modern Maturity,* and you will see the world transformed.

• Fewer species. There will be less variety of living things in 2100 than in 2000 because species are being annihilated faster than they are coming into existence. We don't know yet if this will be merely a shame, a tragedy, or a catastrophe.

• Fewer languages. The number of human languages spoken will decline from about six thousand today to half that number a century from now. Why? Because about three thousand languages spoken today are no longer being learned by children. English will be even more dominant.

• More city dwellers. Half a century ago, less than a third of humanity lived in cities; now half of us do. Two centuries ago, only London had a million people; today, 326 cities have more than a million people, and of these, fourteen have more than ten million. This trend will continue. If these numbers make you dizzy, take a reservoir walk before proceeding.

Slam Dunks

The following will almost certainly happen, but sometimes a slam dunk catches the rim and bounces out quite spectacularly.

• More people. We just passed the six billion mark in October and probably have several more billion to go. Virtually none of this growth will occur in the mid-Hudson Valley. Where will it stop and how many people can the Earth support? No one knows. Most estimates place the Earth's long-term capacity at four to sixteen billion. Some place it as low as one billion. Oops.

• Global warming. The Earth's temperature will rise. The Earth's sea level will rise. Weather will become more violent. If you enjoyed Hurricane Floyd, you're going to love the twenty-first century.

• Computers everywhere. Information technology will continue to drive change in the next century. Let's see—nine billion people, 100 computers per person (mostly embedded in other things), each computer a million times more powerful than today's PC, and all of them interconnected. You can deal with it—you just took a reservoir walk. Keep reading.

Probable

The following will most likely happen.

• More countries. The trend toward more and smaller countries will continue. Since countries rarely merge voluntarily—and the Age of Conquest is over—this is probably a one-way street. The Soviet Union broke into fifteen parts; the Chechnyans would like to make it sixteen. And East Timor could be the thread that unravels the Indonesian batik.

• Longer lives. Average life span will definitely continue to rise. Maximum life span may rise, perhaps spectacularly so. One hundred fifty candles on the cake and still healthy? Imagine going to a club to meet a cute guy and the main competition is your great-grandmother—or your great-granddaughter. Imagine what this will do to actuarial tables.

• Alternative energy arrives. Big time. The basic science and engineering for an energy economy based on nonpolluting, renewable sources may be completed early in the century—say by 2025. We'll stop converting carbon into carbon dioxide by simply burning it, and instead use the precious molecular bonds in our finite supply of fossil fuels to create materials. Global implementation will take most of the century.

• Space exploration. The slow exploration and inhabitation of our solar system will continue, assuming political stability. More probes, more satellites, more orbiting observatories, colonies, and interplanetary travel, along with some new players: China, Japan, Korea, and others.

Possible

The following are wild cards that might happen. They have certainly powered the plots of more than a few technothrillers.

• Nuclear exchange or meltdown. Given the dispersion of nuclear know-how, the disintegration of the former Second World, the number of nuclear weapons extant, the number of persistent enmities, and the number of reactors, it seems entirely possible that we will see at least one more Hiroshima, one more Chernobyl.

• Plague. Biological know-how is expanding and dispersing, too. Imagine a disease that kills like rabies and travels like the flu. Half a billion dead? And you know terrorists will hit the City first. Shun the weekenders.

• First contact. An alien civilization could be detected at any moment, or never. More of us will certainly be listening in the twenty-first century than in the twentieth. You can even join the fun. Go to <http://setiathome.ssl.berkeley.edu/> to help sift through radio emissions from space.

• Really really advanced technologies. Biotechnology, nanotechnology, artificial life. What these will bring—especially in the out years: 2070, 2080, 2090—is beyond my ability even to guess.

Hot, crowded, and overwhelming—not most people's idea of a cheery future. Can't we just go back to the way things were? No, that is one thing we absolutely cannot do. The teeming masses of humanity cannot be fed with nineteenth-century agriculture, the hosts of genies cannot be stuffed back in their bottles, the Internet was designed to survive a nuclear exchange. There is no turning back, there is no standing still.

What does science fiction say about our future? There are three main alternatives.

1. Everything goes wrong. The nukes fly, the crops fail, the robots go berserk and the cockroaches inherit the Earth. A post-apocalyptic, dystopian nightmare plays out on a shattered planet.

This could happen. From On the Beach to Terminator 2, a whole disaster subgenre lays out the many different paths to hell—some ludicrous, some chillingly plausible.

2. Everything goes right. World leaders sit down together and wisdom prevails, family planning becomes universal, technology becomes foolproof, solutions are applied proactively and human beings inherit the Earth.

This could happen, too, but how likely is it? I'll simply note that few utopian novels have been written in the last three-quarters of a century. The writers don't believe in them, and neither do most readers.

3. We try our best to walk forward. There is no turning back, there is no standing still. Walking is controlled falling. With each step, your foot catches you just in time. Try taking a step at a time in the right direction.

This is the only alternative that is both realistic and hopeful. Vote with your ballots, vote with your dollars, vote with your words and deeds. Use the Internet as a fulcrum. Do as little or as much as you can. And remember—

It's either you, or the cockroaches.

About the Author

BRIAN DANA AKERS grew up in Kalamazoo, Michigan and spent his teenage years building telescopes, reading science fiction, and practicing Yoga. He started six years of undergraduate and graduate studies at the University of Michigan in 1975, with his senior year abroad in India. His studies included Sanskrit and Indian history.

Brian then left for the San Francisco Bay Area and worked as a typographer and network manager. In July of 1991—with sun, moon, and earth aligned in the Golfo de California—he met Loretta, moved to New York, and married her.

Today, Brian and Loretta live together happily. He writes science fiction, translated the *Hatha Yoga Pradipika* from the Sanskrit, and founded YogaVidya.com. You can find out more about him at BrianDanaAkers.com.